Note From the Writer:

The electricity that courses young love deeply consumed my mind a little over a year ago. I found it mostly thrilling, hair raising, bright and breezy, while also scary at times. But I have this thing about tragedy. I told myself measuring hands is a frequent thing done in close proximity. Memorizing skin callouses is typical when you're young and unbecoming. I grew fascinated by someone tapping on your shoulder and going unnoticed. I tossed grief into the circle, spinning the wheel endlessly, making a whole story from the gold. And it's all very tragic and real, like great stories are.

I hope you love it the same way you do your dog, or your mom, or that one boy so far-off, gone

—Dawson

"Time turns flames to embers
You'll have new Septembers"

—Taylor Swift

"They'll talk about us, all the lovers
How we kiss and kill each other"

—Ella Yelich-O'Connor

"When the world was at war before
We just kept dancing"

—Lana Del Rey

Chapter 1:

In the Foyer, I Saw That Man with the Straitjacket

IF you read the newspaper often, I'm certain you've read this story already, and you probably find it very boring and old by now, as though it were the first story ever poorly typed out and sold at the nearest drugstore. If you don't read the newspaper, you may have heard this story on the car radio, if you were tuned to the correct station, but also if you ever went to a high school party. It was part of the eulogy at my best friend's funeral, so maybe you heard it even there. It really doesn't matter so much where you got it from. I just hope that you find this version of the story much younger and newer, since I'm the one who lived the whole thing anyway, and I'm telling you how it actually went instead—simple, powerful and intelligent as changing position in a kiss.

So anyway, this story goes a long way back to June 1986, before I spent any time in the madhouse, and it takes place in this goddamned town named Cradock that has just the most boring weather you might ever come to know. Where often you'd get a bridge dedicated to you—only you have to jump it first—when I decided I was at the worst goddamn advantage of anybody ever born in the world's long history. I thought I would start by saying that because you were going to notice soon enough anyway, and you were going to be all surprised when you did, and people were going to see and it was much worse than anything. Don't you know people are very stubborn people? I find they often make everything difficult for the very purpose of nothing at all. I know this better than anybody because my name was deeply flawed in context, on the front pages of the goddamn newspaper at that, and everybody made it this whole grand deal. I have a psychiatrist because of it even. Her name is Phoebe, and she's a very nice lady, who knows everything apparently.

A few weeks ago, Phoebe asked what I wanted to be when I grow up, and before I could answer or anything, she told me I'd make for a very good writer. She said I pay very good attention, and that all the best writers do, apparently. I haven't quite decided if she's wrong or not just yet, but when I do, I'll let you know of course. I have to let you know everything.

Almost over a year ago, my mom died from leukemia, and even though it's almost over a year ago, I feel as though I woke up only yesterday morning to it. I'm very worried I'm going to feel that way forever if I keep thinking about it any, but it's hard to stop myself from doing so. I have tried, though, putting together this very terrible plot that I've let go way too far, but I've found some things are better forgotten about.

Once I found out my mom was dying, I'd wake up having the most uneasy feeling, beginning in my mind and staying quite a while, sharing the whole room with myself. I always thought it to be like an overcast sky, the way it would cloud over, and the noise it made like a gray static wave. I found the only way to make it stop was reading. My favorite thing to read was the newspaper, but you don't have very much freedom deciding that if you're in the madhouse, so I cut out the Ben Coleridge story from the newspaper, and folded it inside my shoe. I hid it in my underwear drawer, thinking nobody would look there anyway, until I found my roommate laying on his cot in just goddamn boxer shorts with the very same paper in his hand. His name was Ansel.

Ansel had a very certain intensity about himself that might scare you at first, but know that although he acted so—he wasn't at all mad. He was probably the smartest person I've ever known instead, having just the finest mind that you could build a whole new city from.

It didn't take long before I noticed Ansel had on my boxer shorts, and so I glared storms at him. He smiled proudly like how a schoolboy reveled in his glory would.

"Wear your own goddamn clothes," I said to him. I had told him this many times already but he just wouldn't listen to anything you said.

"Ease up just a little, Jack," he said. "Do you want those old man wrinkles? No girl would ever touch you looking that way."

He winked at me, and then, as he so often would, he removed my boxers and tossed them up right at me, leaving himself completely naked. You always found Ansel naked and wanting you to look at him. Sometimes, to be honest, I would. I had nothing else to do anyway.

"Have you noticed it's cold today?" he asked, smiling at himself of course.

I ignored him.

"Could I have that?" I asked, talking about the newspaper he was holding. "I didn't say you could read it. It wasn't in your drawer anyway."

"No, you didn't, and alright, yes, it wasn't," he said. "But I didn't think I had to ask you either. You're so uptight sometimes, do you know that? I don't know anybody like you."

"And I don't know anybody like you," I said. "Yet I rarely complain about it how you do."

"Who's Ben Coleridge anyway?" he asked.

"Just somebody that I used to know," I said—though Ben Coleridge was my best friend. I just didn't think Ansel had to know that or anything. Some people shouldn't know everything about you.

"Does Ben involve you having that scar?" he asked, pointing above my lip where I have this scar. Ansel would ask me about it very often, but I never told him what happened or anything. I was just glad to know it wasn't fading any because it's from this terrific memory I have.

"I told you not to ask me about that," I said, although every day I hoped he would.

"I know, but awful pity what happened anyway," he said, looking up at me in some way I wouldn't forget. "Do you think it's a mad world?"

"I do, and somehow I got put in it with you," I said, going over and yanking the paper out from his hands. "How about I pay you something to put some goddamn clothes on?"

"Like you've got money. How about a blowjob?" He asked just about anyone for a blowjob. He didn't know anything about how to behave.

"How about I wash your mouth out with vinegar?" I said.

"Oh, you know I'm only teasing! I bet you don't know how anyway."

I walked over to my drawer to put the paper away. I folded up my underwear he'd worn, and placed the paper neatly beneath it. Once I did that, I made my way to Ansel's dresser to pick him out something to wear. He had only two shirts in his drawer at that moment, although one had a strange stain on it, and so I decided on the cleaner looking one. I went and handed it to him.

"Put that on, please, and find some pants too," I said.

"Fine, but only because you thought to ask nicely," he said, finding some jeans to wear.

I was just standing there while he got dressed, and I can admit that he had some muscle on his stomach. I always wondered where he'd gotten it from, but I ended up not ever knowing.

"Just so you know, I don't have a belt," he said. I looked at him confused.

"But how have you kept your pants up?" I asked. It made absolutely no good sense to me because I can't keep mine up without a goddamn belt on. It's so very annoying.

"I just don't worry about it very much," he told me.

"You have some very interesting mind," I said, going to lay down on my bed, just needing a rest. I tire out pretty easy.

"Are you going to bed already?" he asked, sitting at the end of my bed, and bouncing around on his butt like a kid would.

"It wouldn't be so bad to. I barely sleep anyway with all your snoring in my ear." He snored like crazy. You haven't ever heard anybody snore until you've heard Ansel.

"But you can't go to sleep yet. I want to show you something," he said.

"No, you only want to play around," I said, yawning.

"Please, Jack!" he begged. His bouncing became more increasingly desperate after, and I knew he wouldn't stop anyway, so I sat up and leant back on the metal bedframe. I forgot just how bad those were to lean on. I mean you couldn't relax or anything.

Ansel leant in toward me after.

"I promise you won't regret it," he said, holding out his right pinky finger when he did. I gave him a stare at first and then joined mine to his. It was the only promise Ansel ever made that I knew to be true.

Apparently John Macauley was a shoe salesman until he opened a boys school in September 1945 once the war had ended. Its outside had pure mahogany brick and evergreen treetops nearby that stamped out any smoke the gunfire brought about. Its freshly mowed lawn did the boys good to either study or perhaps lay around on. Had you found enough boys glad to, and there were plenty, rugby on the weekend days. Laughter slowly caught onto the greenery like how a buried ember did a once doused fire, and the war they fought became another memory.

Inside, there was a fancy chandelier and a staircase waxed twice a day. You'd find the ninth stair creaks, or it does now. I don't know whether that was always there. You'd have to ask Ansel about that. He was the one who told me the story anyway.

I followed him through the sunlit corridor.

"Women were dancing without any clothes in the road and the parade wagons were done up with these shiny roses. Fireworks were set for eight o'clock and a jazz band sought order while everyone waited around."

"What were they celebrating?" I asked him.

"War's over, Jack!" he exclaimed. "For a while, there was peace and celebrating. Do you know about peace in 1946?"

"Only what they taught in school," I said.

"You can forget about that. Anything you're told in school is just talk. Because people just talk all the time. Do you get that?" I nodded my head, and so he went on. "Peace in 1946 was just a spectacle, and not a very good one either. Nobody's going to sit through a poorly done spectacle. Radley Peterson was especially angry about it."

"Radley Peterson?" I said. I never knew anybody with that name. "Don't you think Radley's too grown to be a schoolboy's name? You should do Stephen or—"

"No, Radley was his name," he said. "It's not something I just made up."

"Do you mean it's a real story?" I had only asked him that because most stories he told would have something in them so highly colored it gave out what certainty you had. I think it was partly his eyes. He had these real dark green eyes that deceive you.

"I mean exactly that," he said. "Anyway, peace hadn't yet found its way to the Macauley Boys School. At least not to Radley Peterson. Peace to him was a goddamn hoax. Do you want to know why?" he asked, but he gave you no time to answer or anything. I don't think he wanted you to. He got very sore and all when you did anyway.

"He'd shot his best friend in the goddamn head. Some tragic incident that was. His name—damnit! I forgot."

"Is the name that important anyway?" I asked. From saying just that, Ansel was so upset you would have thought I punched him in the stomach.

"Incredibly!" he cried out. "A name's got more to it than you think. I hoped you knew that already. It's what people first know you by. You don't just remember somebody's name, you know. You put it with something."

"Oh, sorry. How about Stephen?" I said.

"Fine, Stephen's fine," he said, turning the corner and gathering speed. "Anyway, war had its downtime and Radley and Stephen would mess around the whole day when it did. Except one day when Radley had to piss and so he went somewhere private to do so. I got told he had a very small penis and so he wouldn't take a goddamn piss around anybody. He was shy about it."

"And who told you that?" I asked.

"Stop cutting in please. You put a whole damper in the story when you do," he said. I told you he got sore. He could be a goddamn child about it.

"I can try not to," I said.

"It's plenty enough to try, just so you know." I heard him smile.

We came down the stairs into the foyer, and I remember the ninth stair creaking because Ansel made some joke about the whiney architecture. "I told you it was one night only!" he said. I think it was a sex joke. He loved those more than anybody.

In the foyer, I saw that man with the straitjacket and some girl dancing alone in the corner nearby.

Ansel pointed at the man. "Apparently that's Radley Peterson," he said, pausing our wandering completely from this fact so very remarkable.

"Have you spoken to him?" I said.

"Oh, well, yes, of course I have. And would you understand why Radley Peterson had a shotgun on him when he went to go piss?" Ansel asked.

I nodded my head.

"No you wouldn't," he said, getting loud. "Radley would have a M1 Garand! You told me some goddamn lie, didn't you!" he screamed at the man. "Radley told me he'd taken a shotgun with him and that Stephen came up right on him and so he shot him thinking he was the enemy. But I mean—that can't be! In war you have to be quick otherwise you're just another dead man. It's why they'd use the M1 Garand. Because it's goddamn clip was easy to reload!"

"Ansel, stop yelling at him. I don't think it matters very much," I said. Looking at the man, helpless and staring at the floor, I knew the story had glossed over in his mind by now. It was so long ago anyway.

Forgetting Radley Peterson in the foyer, we resumed sailing down the hallway, only stopping to gaze out a window.

I remember Ansel putting his hands in his jean pockets like goddamn Westley Reid would do. Westley's a big pain in my ass. He knows just how good looking he is and I don't think anybody like that is honest. I mean you must know plenty about him already. He's quite known for his parties and I even went to a few.

"Stephen and Radley were together, you know" Ansel said.

"Radley told you that?"

"He let it slip that he gave him a handy once." He motioned indecently to demonstrate. "How come you don't ever give me a hand? It's not so foreign, you know."

"Because you're a dirty moron," I said. He just laughed and looked out the window, down below at what green the winter cold hadn't kept, eventually continuing on about some hot day 1945. Summer had already peaked and people would rather spend their picnic days inside in the cool air.

"You weren't given that luxury were you a soldier," Ansel said. "You wore your khaki cotton and didn't complain a goddamn bit about it. Although you couldn't since you've got no time anyway." Ansel's voice was steadying out as he spoke more on the war. War to Ansel, really, was no joke at all. Haunting him greatly in ways I never knew about. "So Radley had gone out for a piss deep in the forest woods so nobody'd find out about his tiny penis. You wouldn't want anyone to know about your tiny penis, would you? I know you've got one."

"Wouldn't you like to know?" I asked, playing alongside the color set alight in his voice.

"So there Radley was—out somewhere in the greenwood amidst his ever so quiet piss. He didn't know that Stephen followed him, or that's what he said anyway. But wouldn't you notice somebody on you—when you're in a war at that? I know I would anyway. Somehow Radley didn't, though, not until Stephen came up and jumped on him as a clean joke. Radley thought he was the enemy so he put one right in his forehead. Shot him dead."

"And so you think he did it knowingly?"

"I do, yes! Do you know how glad I am that you asked?" I knew plenty alright. "Because Radley had told me he'd used a shotgun but you and I know just how the M1 Garand was right at his disposal. He's a filthy, goddamned liar and probably forever at that."

"But why would he do that anyway? Didn't you say they were having a love affair?

"Precisely! Since you asked me, Stephen had a girl at home that would send him naked photographs and Radley found one and went crazy about it. I think so, at least. It's only plausible."

"How's that plausible?" I asked.

"Do you have another reason for him?"

"He might just be plain mad," I said. "And maybe he shot his best friend in the head just to do it. You know you don't have to put out a good excuse for everybody."

Ansel shrugged at me.

"It doesn't matter anyway. He was already a strange boy, and once people got word that he'd shot Stephen, there was almost no way out for him," Ansel said. "He came back from the war to a world completely alone. Even his parents didn't love him anymore, and so away he went, set off absolutely on the worst backdraft current to the Macauley School For Boys."

"But that was only right, I mean, he shot Stephen on purpose. You can't just do that anyway," I said.

"People don't have the mind you and I do, Jack. Nobody thought he'd shot his best friend on goddamn purpose. Radley hadn't told about his and Stephen's involvement anyway. It was just a tragic incident to everybody and in time just another war casualty. Radley lost his goddamn marbles about it. Peace wasn't for his liking any. And so that's why, at precisely eight o'clock that July fourth night in 1946, Radley Peterson cut some boy's throat straight open."

Ansel slowly drew his finger around his throat like it was a camp story wearying out the bedding.

"He told me nobody knew about war and that's why he did it. I told him most people don't care to know anything they don't need to," Ansel said. "Most people wanted John Macauley in jail for allowing Radley admittance despite his background in the war. So John ended up selling the school to the county instead, and they made it into a goddamn sanitorium. Radley would've gotten sent to the state penitentiary otherwise. Keeping the Macauley name was part of the agreement."

Some areas were closed away when John sold because they had no use anymore, like the indoor pool, and so it got drained. I always found that annoying because I wouldn't have minded a nice swim every once in a while. Oh, and the squash courts too. I only played squash one time anyway so that meant almost nothing to me. But often I read, and so I was devastated to hear Ansel say the library got closed too!

"Radley told me about this place," he said, snapping his fingers like his own words distracted him just enough to forget about a war he played no right hand in. And so the destination we'd so lazily come for had given out.

Ansel had brought me to the library.

It wasn't very big, only about eight feet by twenty feet wide inside. There was a chess set that had a black knight on its side, and a spider's cobweb up in the corner that Ansel declared too high to clean out. It had a window also that didn't open because the wood around it had grown too old. Although I don't know that it was meant to be opened anyway. It's a long way down.

I remember there being a table lamp without a shade or lightbulb, and a world globe that Ansel found great enjoyment in. He'd spin it around and spin it around and in his own tune would put on for you that "I Feel the Earth Move" song. Listen closely enough and maybe you could.

On my right, there was a study carrel with a pen drawing on it of a two story house with porch steps leading up to a front door that didn't have a door handle.

"Did you draw that?" I asked Ansel. I thought he must have. It didn't have any fingermarks on it, and you just don't survive time all that easily.

"Maisie did," he said. He was over by the globe. "Don't you think she's good? I couldn't even draw a bird probably."

"Have you brought Maisie here?" I asked.

"I have before. I mean you know how she is anyway. Doesn't like to stay in one place very long."

"I know," I said. I'd known Maisie Kenton longer than him. "She forgot the doorknob."

"I don't know that she's done with it yet."

I didn't say it, but it had looked very done to me and that's just what put me down about it—how a doorknob there didn't quite belong. One hardly ever does anyway.

I looked at Ansel having found a mantel clock to occupy his hands.

"Won't you just look at that?" he said. It was broken, the clock of course. "It doesn't work anymore. Do you think it ever did?" He was pretty upset about it. I don't know why.

"It probably did at one time. I mean it's older than you and I put together anyway," I said to lighten him up, but he was too amused by the clock piece to acknowledge that I had.

"Do you want to know something? I hardly believe in time. Don't you think it's one big illusion?" he said. I just did a shrug. You had to just shrug at Ansel sometimes when he got that way. I don't know what quite. Something blue, though.

So yes, it was a rather tiny room for a library to be in. You'd hardly even believe it was a library at first. I would have thought maybe it was a janitor's storehouse if Ansel hadn't shown me the glass door that opened into a lonely bookcase. It was nearly empty with, I'd say, only forty books inside it. I read about two a day.

But anyway, I was in the library one morning when achingly I had come to realize I'd read every book in there.

I thought at first certainly there was no way I could have done that. I wondered if it were possible that I could be that violently bored, and the wondering gave me a headache from just doing so, meaning that I didn't have long—oh yes, not very long now until my mind would slip into the neighborly pothole it had that first brought me there. And so I thought perhaps I could break the window open with my head and jump out from it, down onto the grass underneath, but yet, that seemed almost boring to do, and I didn't want to stain another shirt either. I would have stayed in the library until my eyes grew tired enough to just close forever but I couldn't have! Dad was coming to visit that day. Instead, resigning defeat from every idea I had, I sat down on the carpet, and when I did, a book from the very top ledge tumbled right down onto my shoulder. I opened it of course, but only to find it entirely blank instead. And then it turned to fine dust in my hands!

I sat dearly with this occurrence for a couple of weeks at first, just so you know, until I forgot to close the blinds. I mean those goddamn venetians blinds are hard enough to close anyway. And so instead, I woke up early one morning because the sun had poured into the room, thinly, like how river water does, burning right over my eyes. I opened them, remembering June when I did, and decided to never remember anything ever again. And so came today, so wondrously I almost hadn't recognized the plot I'd once fit so happily together.

I put my bicycle lock on and breathed right in the rosemary air Paton Street has to give out. You might think it's just another empty town street and while it is, yes, Phoebe's little working place is also right there on the corner and every Monday, around three o'clock, you could find me down it. Likely blinking out what tired expressions I hadn't caught in the mirror faced door at home.

I knocked on the door once. Phoebe parted the blind slats and smiled. She opened the door and I walked inside, first noticing the violet paint over that just smothers you entirely. I don't know why she chose that color but I also haven't ever asked. Someday I might if I remember to.

I sat down on the dark, graying couch she has, and stared at the rather strange oil painting she has right behind her desk. She told me once that it was her great uncle. It's a brightly colored pea green, yet somehow there's a creepy despair to it. Every time you look up, he's just there. Him and his cruel stare that makes you think you don't belong. And maybe that's because you don't.

I looked away at the burgundy flowerpot with a sole foxglove in it, placed just right on the window to where the sunlight comes in. Phoebe had bought that because I told her foxgloves were easy to care for, and they are. It would have to be my favorite part of the whole place because my mom used to garden. She owned a flower stand on Ebury Street even, but sold it away to somebody when she got sick. So that's how I know about foxgloves, and flowers mostly. My mom's favorites were those pretty white tulips.

Beside that is a dream catcher and a wax candle in a jar.

"May I ask how you're feeling today, Jack?"

Phoebe's voice was awfully quiet, seeming nervous almost.

"You just have, and don't say that you haven't," I said, cozying myself on that couch I told you about before.

Phoebe had gone over to her desk right then, and opened the very top drawer that usually gave her trouble to open, except for today when it just hadn't. I found it strange of course.

But anyway, she stayed there behind her desk, near the drawer.

I looked away for a moment, and over at her windowsill where a bird, plump and blue, had now settled cozily onto the outside ledge. I was looking

19

around for you, I would have told him, but the window was closed and I couldn't quite do anything about that. Might you wait for me—the silver bike right out front is mine. I thought we could find another way home, and perhaps I could forgive you also. I know you didn't mean to forget me.

You couldn't have.

I looked back over at Phoebe behind the desk, noticing she had placed one hand inside the drawer. I thought maybe she had a thirty eight in there ready to put my mind to sleep forever, but it was hardly that.

"—I have this for you," she said, taking something out bandaged in newspaper. "I hope you'll like it."

She came around her desk, not bothering to close the drawer, and came over to me, handing the gift over when she did.

I turned it over in both my hands, gently wrinkling the newspaper covering while I did. My mind did its ordinary wandering. I was a house mouse again and impossibly happy about it.

Steady, I unwrapped the tape she put onto the paper. I didn't want to rip it or anything when it could have your story on it. Perhaps I could read about you later today.

Once I finished taking off the last tape piece, I only had to remove the newspaper around it now. I did that like my mom's finest China was parceled up inside, revealing a blue leather journal when I did. I hope it's a faux leather and isn't very expensive or I'd feel terrible about it then.

"I remember you said you liked the color blue," Phoebe said. It would have to be my favorite color probably.

"But what's it for?" I asked, admiring the journal in all its terrific blue magnificence.

"You're a very clever boy, Jack. I hoped we could use that cleverness in working towards your memory retention. Do you remember how I said you'd make for a very good writer?" Phoebe asked.

I nodded, looking at her of course, and I smiled at finding what I must do instead.

First, though, you should know my name is Jack Boyd. That's more important than anything.

But I'm certain you won't forget anyway.

Chapter 2:

ANOTHER BOY JUMPS IN RIVER

Mostly nothing can surprise me at all today, not since I woke up to my new roommate, Sawyer, biting down into my arm's skin. He was goddamn mad! I knew by those eyes he had. He didn't have those warm green eyes Ansel did. His were these pale blue and dead. But strangely, him biting didn't hurt or anything, though I did bleed onto the bed linen a whole lot. I slept right until noon after, and was only woken because a nurse was screaming terribly.

I broke that same arm on this swing when I was a goddamn kid too. My neighbors hadn't yet labeled me mad, so I felt it completely well enough. I remember it in the way you do receiving your first pocket money on your birthday. It might be my first memory even.

It was barely autumn. You can recognize late September by how the leaves whistle just right, kindly to the wind. There was a new wooden swing set in the park, so popular among every kid too. My best friend Ben was most excited about it, and I tried hard to be. I don't like heights, just so you know. But that didn't matter. I'd once do anything Ben did.

I flew off the swing. I hit the Earth pretty hard, tearing my cheek up and tasting my own blood, putting a dirty nickel on my tongue. I can't seem to forget that, or the snapping noise my arm made when it broke in half. If you lick your middle finger, put your thumb to it and do a snap, that's exactly how it sounded.

I don't know how long I was out for. You could hit me gently and I'd be out for a while. A tiny bug was there in my ear whispering chaos you'd only recognize late spring. I saw the grassy field that goes out past the park into the forest pine branches. And I swore there were daisy flowers too, but I couldn't find them today. I gave up looking around only to watch the sunset. I hope you got outside to see it or put your nearest window to some good abuse. It exploded out in those colors that make you wonder. But each day now breaks the same. And those colors are just plain boring. I think so, at least.

I had a blue cast put on. Ben was the first person who signed it. He thought it was so neat. He tried breaking his own arm in two even. But he never could. And I never could quite understand why he wanted to. I don't think he meant anything bad, but I don't know. Ben was the best friend I ever had and yet somehow, I'd known almost nothing about him.

His favorite color was light red. He liked playing that Centipede game at the arcade and swimming in the creek. He never got nervous around girls. He wanted to be on television, but he didn't want to be too famous or anything. Just enough to where somebody might notice him in the grocery line was his dream.

Once I had a dog whose leash caught onto the fence when I was only eight. His name was Russ. He was a chocolate Labrador Retriever and had the prettiest coat you ever saw on a dog.

I won't ever forget it. I was at home alone with him, and he kept whimpering at the back door. I wasn't supposed to take him outside with nobody there. But he wouldn't stop and I was just feeling terrible about it and my dad got mad when he'd pee in the house so I thought I should anyway.

I don't know what the leash caught on. My dad said a nail, though I don't remember a nail being there. I do remember the noise Russ made like he had a sick person's bad cough. I hear it sometimes in the distance of bad dreams I have.

I couldn't undo the buckle on it. I don't know if I tried hard enough anyway. I was only eight.

He ended up choking himself to death if you hadn't realized that already. I had to sit there and watch him die because I didn't want to leave him. I just wouldn't do that. I told him I was sorry, we shouldn't have gone outside, and how I couldn't do anything. I don't know whether he even heard me. But I really need to believe he did.

My parents came home and found me asleep in the grass with him. He loved that grass very much. I hope what they say about dogs and heaven is true and that it's a better world and there's enough grass up there for him. I hope he's not alone either. I hope he found my mom. I know she'd really like that because she wouldn't want to be alone either.

We buried him right in the backyard with his favorite toy and treat box. I dreamt about him for a long while until that became only nightmares instead. And I began to hear him whimpering at my closed bedroom door. I haven't told anyone but you that part. I hope that's alright.

Anyway, I am writing this because I've only just found out about Norman Bauer and I wasn't surprised or anything.

I read about it in the paper, you know, where you can read about everything nowadays. ANOTHER BOY JUMPS IN RIVER was the heading. It was dated October 1ˢᵗ, 1986.

"17-year-old boy, Norman Bauer, caught in deep river stream was drowned yesterday morning."

It seemed to be quite the story, so you might have already heard about him somewhere. But I knew Norman sometimes from around school. And nobody ever thought to ask me anything. People never do.

Norman was quiet. His hair wasn't ever combed, and he always had that tired look about his face like he never knew how to sleep. He got you down just by looking at him. I had home economics with him and he'd just stare right at the floor too. But not in a sad way or anything. It was just something he'd do.

"Norman was said to have jumped into the water calmly by those onlooking. I thought maybe it was him being a boy, you know how boys are today, said one neighbor." I feel terribly sorry for that neighbor knowing not a plain thing about boys! Even sorrier that I know almost everything.

Oh, but anyway. Norman's resuscitation was quite impossible to do. And so he laid there, up on that riverbank, eyes white and wide open—dead.

Honestly, you shouldn't go about saving everybody anyway.

Chapter 3:

Don't Kill the Snail

I remember it was a very bright and evergreen day and the sky had that glazed dryer sheet look to it that either meant the summer was there already, or nearing. I'd just finished my tenth whole year in school, and the paper boy hadn't yet joined those other missing persons. He would be found dead, yes, however not for some long while so not quite worth your excitement right now. Stop that anyway.

Earlier that day, Ben and I were at Eisner's, that drugstore on Felix Street. Most probably to buy a Coke and fool around. Isn't summer for that anyway?

I know you wouldn't think a drugstore would be a common place to hang around but there was this pretty girl behind the cash desk. Ben thought so at least. Her name was Marigold. I was too glad noticing the working air conditioner, and that day Ralph Macchio on the magazine aisle.

"I don't think she's working today," Ben said.

"Must be at home," I said. But the funny part was, Ben already knew that. I mean that he liked Marigold a whole lot. "I know you've got her schedule memorized anyway. Don't say you don't."

"Oh, shut up," he said. "Don't be funny. What are you looking at anyway?" he asked, pushing me aside.

"Ralph Macchio? Wasn't he was in that one movie we saw at the Colony?"

"He's the karate kid, too," I said.

"When does that come out?" he asked.

"Next week, I think."

"Oh, that's pretty close!" he said, giving that particular smile I can't ever do right on paper.

Later that same day, I was sitting on Ben's bed and he was on the floor wearing no shirt—that was instead straightened and braced for its peculiar demise.

"Don't you think you'd better use scissors?" I asked because rather decidedly, he'd employed the pocket knife we'd once found inside my dad's old tool bag. I gave it to him for his birthday that same year.

"I haven't got some nearby," he said, beginning to cut along the right sleeve. "Besides, I think I can make it work. Have even a little faith, Jack! I swear you won't hurt anybody."

"Oh you don't know that!" I said delightedly, lying down on the bed.

"I know a whole lot more than I let out," he said. "Remember at the arcade I asked you how to pass by that mutant swarm on Stargate?" I never really enjoyed that game. It's so goddamn hard anyway. "You had to let them come right to you first. I knew that already cause I'd beaten that level before."

"So why did you ask me?"

"Because I just felt like asking you. You were being too quiet that day anyway, if I remember correctly—" he paused, seemingly to consider his own reliability "—and I'm fairly certain I do." He was fairly certain about nearly everything. I liked that about him. "Remember Westley taught me to whistle? But I could whistle before I met you even!"

"So you're just terrible?"

"I would hope not. Do you think I am?" he said innocently. I was feeling sorry, so I sat up on my elbow and looked at him.

"I think you're alright," I told him.

"Jack Boyd thinks I'm alright! I don't need anything more in life honestly." He smiled quietly at the floor. "But don't start crying or anything."

"You're mad. I was hardly about to do that."

"I wouldn't mention it to anybody if you did," he said, holding up the cut through shirt, admiring it altogether like it was his Don Mattingly rookie card, but that was safe in the glass box right above his bed of course. "Are you ready?"

"For what?" I asked him.

"Ambrose." He began putting the newly designed shirt on.

"What about Ambrose?"

"Marigold lives down there."

"How do you know that even?"

"She said it once. You'd know that if you weren't so busy over in the magazine aisle."

"What, are you a funny man now?"

"It comes pretty easy," he said. "But listen, and don't be a pain in the ass. Also, don't be a sort of wise guy either."

"Oh, relax, won't you?"

"I couldn't do that."

"You're just being plain outright stupid then," I said. "I know you like Marigold, and don't think she doesn't know it either. So you don't have to piss in your drawers about it."

"I'm not pissing my—"

"But you are! And you have to cut it out! What are you scared about anyway? She probably likes you too."

"You can't know that."

"I do because she would've already told the cops about you if she didn't. You're goddamn creepy about it sometimes. You give it almost too much thought. It's like you've got a bad disease or something. You—"

"Had enough?"

"No, although thanks for asking. You act like you're horribly unattractive and you're not or anything. So I won't pity you about it."

Looking over to me, Ben said, "Do you want me to whistle now? Is that what this is about?"

"Oh I don't know why I bothered even! You've got an empty head, I just forgot."

He would have known I meant that jokingly and I might have—but also, in some very terrible way, I was only hoping he would have some go at me. I'd long desired it. I'd gone down Harwich Boulevard for it even. But I found absolutely nothing to occupy this dangerous mind. People are so evil at heart, though certainly you must know that already. But if I'm very honest, I don't think Ben had that badness about him. And please, you have got to believe me. I was the huntsman anyway. You hardly did a simple thing but read between my words. And they are so poorly written. Maybe that is your misreckoning. Oh, I don't know. What am I saying even? Oh, I don't know.

"Do you honestly think she likes me?" Ben asked and that being so, set aside my childish scheming.

"I'd believe it, yes," I said to him. I used to believe in about everything—ghosts even, but I must have grown up sometime later in that day. I'm just noticing that now.

Anyway, Ben and I were headed down toward Ambrose, studying the concrete and its bad temperament—possibly worser than the weather that day. It was brighter than ever, I mean, and raining lightly too. But the sky lost that so quickly like it was barely his to begin. How sorry I'd feel for him—had the fist that drew the hazy cover not belonged to me.

"Are we expecting her outside?" I asked Ben while
counting crevices the pavement would brag about
could it speak.

"Don't know yet," he said. "She might be outside."

"Are you knocking on her door if she's not?"

"I don't know."

"But I remember earlier you saying you knew a lot!
Don't you remember!" I would have hit my jaw for
talking that way, but do you know what he did? He only
laughed, sweeping up what smokestack debris was
around you. But his laugh was often dangerous too,
and told you something about how you are the worst
thing in this world.

"I may knock on her door," he said. "May not. I may
keep walking past—"

"Oh, stop that. We're not coming this whole way for
you to make jokes. What are you going to talk about
anyway? I hope you have something ready in mind."

"I'm working on it."

"But we're almost there now! What do you mean
you're working on it! Are you fooling me? Say you're
fooling me."

"Do you think I am?"

I looked over at him and he was smiling that
goddamned smile that got on my nerves some days.
Ben had this James Dean look about him that most
girls went absolutely mad for. Although I don't think

he knew that even. He had this dirty blonde hair that he kept neatly trimmed and nice hazel eyes.

"You're so darling," I said, shaking my head at him of course.

"That so?" Ben asked.

"Hardly, but my thanks again for—"

"Don't step there," he said abruptly, looming from the blue. He put his hand out to stop my walking and pointed. Down there on the sidewalk alone was this brown little helpless snail. "Don't kill the snail."

"I didn't want to anyway," I said. He bent down onto his right knee to save it and he did so gently that he could have taken the whole day. I remember thinking he was too young to be so neighborly, too sincere. Had a fly ever landed on Ben's fingertip with two broken wings, inviting him in on its misery's end—he'd instead come up with some way to patch them both and blow it a kiss too. It'd fly again, I promise you. Most things do.

We got to Ambrose and Ben was lucky enough because Marigold was outside in her front yard, tossing a disc around with another pretty girl. Both had dotted pink, white and red swimwear on and the lawn sprinkler was on too. It was a boy's dream.

Marigold's quite a sight honestly. She has light brown hair that goes down close by her shoulders, but that day she had it up in a hair ribbon. She was on the cheerleading team at school so I mean that wasn't abnormal or anything. But she isn't now. So don't buy a game ticket.

She's nice too, and she listens when you talk. She doesn't act like she's listening. I hate people who do that. She kisses pretty well, too. I kissed her in a spin the bottle game and she's not rough about it like some girls are. But it didn't mean anything romantic. Party games don't.

I knew the other girl. She was in our year. I saw her at school a lot but I'd never talked to her or anything much, until that day at least. She was the kind of pretty you'd act clumsily around. And I did. But I didn't know a girl could be that nice looking even. I want you to think about the prettiest girl you know until you're staring mad at nothing and blinking desperately at your name.

I never saw anyone like Maisie Kenton and I've since looked around, washing teacup dishes, at the day long tea I rinse down the sink drain. I'd take a bike ride down to the river, put out a quilt, maybe peel a tangerine and read a Sylvia poem. But why should I bother? I am not fleece and I am not young. Maisie Kenton is missing anyway. Oh, but should I use that word?

"Are you boys taking a picture?" Marigold asked. She'd noticed Ben and I standing there like goddamn pet rabbits.

"You're terrible if you are," Maisie said while adjusting the shoulder part on her swimsuit over some.

"I beg your pardon?" Ben said purposely loud, waving dumbly at his ear. "Sorry—I can't hear you that faraway!" But I remember hearing them just fine.

"You shouldn't beg," said Marigold. "It's not that good a look on you. How old are you anyway?"

"Old enough," he said and he did that goddamned smile too.

"Don't be a smart aleck," she said. "When you already know how I feel about that." She made her way to the sidewalk and up to Ben, who got a kiss on his cheek. Maisie stayed behind, looking depressed. "Hi there, Jack."

"Hi there, Marigold," I said like a child mocking his parents would. I didn't mean to sound that way or anything bad. I just used to mess around a whole lot. "How's your day?"

"It's nice." She smiled and sighed. "I almost had nothing to do earlier until I remembered I have a house phone and so I rang Maisie and I told her to come over please, it's dire. I was feeling so dreadful. I could have slept from the boredom. Do you ever have that?"

"Mm don't ask me that," I said, yawning. "Now look what you did."

"Ha!" She laughed. "Isn't that just strange? I love it. Would you have a mint on you, Ben?"

"I don't," Ben said. "Did you expect me to?"

"Oh, no. I didn't. Have you cut your shirt? I liked it fine before." I watched her eyes trace along Ben's exposed biceps and knew she was telling a lie. "So what's new?"

"Jack and I were heading to swim at the creek," Ben answered in this rough, candid demeanor. I didn't know quite about that yet, until then, but I kept my appearance straight anyway. I'm this good actor somewhat. I used to do the school plays even.

"But you don't have swim shorts on?"

"We don't need those, really."

"But what do you swim in?"

"Mostly our boxer shorts." She laughed at that.

"Oh, my!—" she paused and stared at Ben troubledly "—oh, were you not joking? Don't you have a swimsuit?"

"I do but it's not ever that fun wearing it," he said.

"You both are crazy—" she turned slightly behind her "—Maisie won't you come and listen?" Maisie was in the yard, swaying nervously—miserably, even. She came up beside Marigold.

"What is it?" she asked. She has this kind, timid voice. Her parents are from some rural town in England and so that's why. I think it's nice and lovely and I'd put it in a music box if somehow I could.

"Boys wear boxer shorts when they swim!" Marigold said, laughing. Maisie looked over at me.

"What's your name?" she asked, drowning out the sprinklers humming in the yard doing so. I had this dream that very same night about a silver teakettle pot I had put on the stove that whistled out nothing but that simple question. It so quickly became a nightmare when the radioman started asking me too. And the newshound on a ladder at my bedroom window scraping the glass. So I ran to wake my parents up only to find them gone instead, leaving behind a sticky notepad that had on it the very same thing.

Sometimes I'd rather do anything but dream.

"I'm Jack," I said flatly to Maisie. I was feeling so hot, I remember. I burn up so terribly around girls, honestly. I'd be plenty alright in a snowstorm without my topcoat if there was a girl around.

"And do you wear your trousers while out for a swim, Jack?" she asked, looking amazed.

"I mean why not!" Ben interrupted. "You girls are too old schooled. Your clothes are meant to be dirtied, it's what they're for."

"What a spirit you have!" Marigold said, smiling apparently. She was strikingly positive always, even on a cold day. And she spoke her mind admirably. Ben liked that a lot. He just liked her a very great deal really. Loved her, maybe even. I never got around to asking.

"We're teasing you!" Maisie said. "Can't you tease anymore?" She kept looking at me and I couldn't quite decide whether she awaited some overly vague counter, or was trying only to decipher our similarity. She smiled.

"Did you want to come?" I asked from the alleyway like a madman would. It scared me even. "Marigold, you said you were bored anyway."

"Oh, that'd be wonderful!" she said. "Is that alright, Maisie, would you like to?" Maisie noticeably thought it over, crossing her arms and stroking her elbow.

"I'd have to stop by my house for pantyhose," she said. "But afterward, I'd be delighted to join—oh, I'm just teasing!"

I smiled. Ben laughed and Marigold said, "I have to just put the sprinkler away first. Ben, would you mind? I could use your help. It won't take even a minute."

"I don't mind," he said. With that, they disappeared up the yard.

"So you're very quiet," Maisie said to me. I looked right at her. "Do you nod at least?" I nodded yes, stupidly. "What are you in the eleventh grade now?" I nodded once more, yes. "So won't you act grown?"

I thought perhaps the sun had dehydrated me so badly I misheard! I hadn't known someone could speak that goddamn plain to you until the day I met Ansel!

My mouth was slightly ajar at first in just complete surprise. I didn't quite know what to say. It's remained mostly that I never do anyway.

"Oh—I'm sorry," I said, looking crazily at the backdrop homes for any sort of little dull word that just might do.

"Don't say that word for nothing."

"But I only meant—"

"And don't you look at my hips either."

"I wasn't," I told her.

"I never said that you were. I was only asking that you don't."

"But I wouldn't anyway."

"So do you mean I have misshapen hips?"

"I don't mean that, sorry—"

"I'm just teasing, Jack! I was only trying to wind you up further. I thought I'd made it obvious. Look at my hips all you need." She was absolutely mad.

"You don't make very good sense," I said.

"And you don't quite know how to be around a girl!" She smiled again, and so I did too.

I look back on this and just remember the sunlight so blonde and clean. It's strange almost because I didn't know it'd one day become this great memory to write about. Curious, curious time. So fantastically deviant in its best tie too.

At the sound of Ben's voice, I looked over to notice him and Marigold making their way over. He was of course talking it up about that snail we saw earlier. "It was just right there on the sidewalk," he said. "And Jack was about to step down on it too."

"I wasn't purposely," I cut in, displeased at him for leaving that out. "I didn't know it was there."

"Luckily you had me to warn you, or it'd be caught in your shoe," he said gladly.

"Oh and it's so hard to clean your soles," Marigold said. "I just hate to step in gum for that very reason. How I wish people would learn to hold onto their wrappers. I put mine in my pocket."

"Do you honestly?" I asked.

"I do!" she exclaimed in that way girls do when they're so into something.

"I wouldn't have thought about that," I said. "I don't like chewing gum all that much anyway." I meant that, too. It hurts my jaw.

"Oh, what don't you like about it?" she asked. Marigold looks just about everywhere for reasonings. She really does—or she did anyway, I don't know. I gave up completely on that. She might have too. Some games are too outplayed and over time you come to find no more use in them. But that's for you to learn about on your own.

"I mean it's alright," I said. I don't know why, but I began this feeling sad about our whole conversation. I would have thought my footsteps harmed the garden but they hadn't. And so I can't describe it because there's nothing quite there. I was just glad Maisie waltzed her way in.

"I'm afraid Jack doesn't like very much," she said. "He gave me this earful about my hips while you both were gone."

"Oh that was a misunderstanding!" I said.

"I don't quite remember it that way. Isn't that tough?" She frowned pitiably at me.

"Won't you act grown?" I said, only taunting her of course.

"Oh well, that's not worth anything. I've gotten that from you already."

"Have you?"

"I have, yes. You're so very easy to learn."

"I had better work on that some then."

Maisie's a great conversationalist really. I never once got bored talking to her. Even with her family being wealthy, too. I mean that it's mostly wealthy people who don't know about keeping a conversation, or I think so at least. Have a conversation once with Westley Reid and you'd understand exactly what I mean. He must have grown up totally alone or something.

In time we started out for the creek. Maisie and I talked the whole way about nearly everything possible. She enjoys reading old poetry and sometimes Russian poetry too. Sylvia Plath is her favorite poet. I told her I'd never read much into poetry and she said that was because I was a boy. I didn't know that had anything to do with how you read poetry. So that night, I went home and read my first real poem, or I tried to anyway. "Poppies in October" by Sylvia Plath. I thought it was very good but also sad. You've got to read it sometime.

I never told Maisie I did that, though. I just got nervous about it. I don't know why that was really. I regret my mind so very often.

And so perhaps I should just be honest. I know I hardly ever am but I've saved you from such unnecessary wandering. So do not crawl back, your knees bleeding, and blame me for not warning you. I have, I have, I have.

<u>Chapter 4</u>:

The Most Random, Worrying Case of a Possible Winter Storm

When you are a kid, you do not yet know anything about fine China, and so you might use your mother's finest China for a tea party or a water glass even. You are too preoccupied being a kid to worry about fine China anyway. And so one day, you drop it and it breaks perfectly into a thousand pieces, and you cry and your mother looks quickly only for the broom because there is glass everywhere of course.

Now you are grown. And you have broken a champagne glass. You cry only because your mother is dead. But nothing more about that—wipe your tears and find the broom already. Once you do this, notice in the dustpan how bright the remnants are. So bright they're stunning. Broken glass is so very beautiful. And you've known it for some time. Realize again, you are grown.

"Could you stop that?" I asked Ansel. He was humming. "What song is that anyway?"

"Suzanne," he said. "Haven't you ever heard it?"

"I don't have to. You hum it just about every day."

"And I don't hum for just anybody so you're the luckiest kid I ever met! Did you know that? Luckiest kid I ever met."

He had a spin top and was spinning it around on the floor. He'd stolen it from the drawing room. And he was humming still.

"It's snowing, you know," I said.

"Is it winter already?" he asked. "How come nobody told me?"

I was looking out the window at the snow when I'd noticed this yellow taxi cab driving up the road, slowly making way. Lousy taximen, I thought. And nothing more.

"Don't you want to go outside?" I asked him.

"Is this why you have your shoes on?" he said.

I looked down at my feet. I did have them on. But I couldn't seem to remember doing that. And I don't know why really, but I was very embarrassed he noticed this.

"No, it's dirty flooring in here and I only have white socks," I said, completely making that up.

"Oh goddamn it!" Ansel said abruptly. I never knew what this was about, but he'd do it so often. "I just remembered I'm in the bughouse."

"It's not so bad," I said.

"Do you honestly believe that?" he asked, getting up and going quickly over to his dresser. He seemed frightened almost, doing that.

"Are you alright?" I asked. He was looking steadily in his dresser mirror, eager perhaps for his opponent to move.

"I've lost weight," he said. "Have you noticed that?"

I hadn't, honestly. So I went to have a look myself and when I did, about midway there, I felt a chestnut underneath my shoe. It sounded about that way at least. But instead, I looked down to find Ansel's spin top broken into four separate pieces. So I'd finally done it.

I'd killed the snail.

"I'm sorry," I said. "I really didn't mean to."

I bent down right away to attend my dying friend. I'd done this once before, certainly I could do it again. But I was terribly mistaken.

My hands were covered in blood from the glass. I have glass in my hands. It's my mother's fine China, and I shouldn't have used it, I know that. But please, I couldn't stop the blood. My hands were shaking badly and I knew nothing about how to stop the blood anyway.

I ran the whole way to the police station completely barefooted, and the policeman kept asking me where my shoes were. I don't remember where I've put my shoes, really, I said. I was dancing in the front yard and I must have forgotten them. But please stop asking me about that.

My friend is dead.

I began to scream. I don't remember for how long but I didn't lose my voice to it so not very long of course. What behavior I used to have.

Ansel didn't mind the screaming. He came and sat quietly beside me instead and sat that way until I found someplace to stop. Once I did, he told me about his little brother who carried a horseshoe around wherever he'd go.

"I don't know where he got it!" he said, laughing. "He just had it one day. He'd take it goddamn everywhere. Have it at the dinner table often. And one day when he got home from the school bus—he was two grades below me so we didn't ride the same school bus—but when he got home, his lip was all sort of busted open and purple. So I asked him, what happened? And do you know what he did? He just smiled at me and went up to his room! I only found out later that day when his teacher called my parents that some kid tried taking the horseshoe from him and so my brother broke the kid's nose with it." It seemed he would laugh at this, but he didn't. He frowned instead. I only felt more sorry and depressed.

"Does he have it still?" I asked.

"I bet that he does," Ansel said, looking at me. I remember his eyes so very green like a wild thing, distracting me from tragedy for the first time in a very long time. For just a moment, he made the outside world go entirely quiet. I wish you knew him so you could understand what I mean exactly.

"Don't go all blue on me, Jack."

"I could try not to," I told him. Now I was smiling.

"It's plenty enough to just try," he said. He was smiling also.

I had a crazy thought, but for only a dull second because its subtle whispering was ceased by the doorknob turning. I could hear a tree sway and a choir bird sing tiredly. Shouldn't they know another song by now?

It was an orderly. She was brand new. She stared emptily at first like a stupid adult would and then spoke. And this interested me very much, her not taking only a quick glance and leaving. What was she told?

"Hi, boys. I don't mean to interrupt. I'm doing checks."

At once I noticed her posture. I hadn't meant to, but it was almost impossible to simply reject. It was just terrible. I never saw anyone with such bad posture. She must have spent every working day at a wooden desk, on a stool, in the freezing cold without a wool hat or coat to accompany her. I felt sorry for her. I really did.

"Do you have a cigarette on you?" Ansel asked her.

"Do I have a cigarette?" she repeated. I wish I could have told her not to do this. Ansel hated when you repeated him.

"You've got a pretty mouth," he said. I should have said something but the trouble was her posture. I just couldn't look away. "Did you know that?"

"Oh, thank you," she said in this quiet voice. She smiled but you knew she was embarrassed about it. Her face got so red, and then she scratched around her collarbone.

"So how about a blowjob?" he asked.

I should have leant over and smacked his mouth now that I'm thinking about it, but I didn't of course. I just played it nice.

"Excuse me?" she said. She was not happy at all.

"He doesn't mean that," I said. "He's had a rough day. I broke his spin top just before you came in. It was a terrible accident. You have to forgive him."

I was hoping to distract her with this fact but it didn't quite matter really. She was very angry and you can hardly do anything once someone's angry. And not only that, but adults aren't reasonable enough anyway. Often they find themselves too busy in their activities to enjoy little young things like the noise water flowing makes or how the daylight breaks.

"What's your name, young man?" I'd never heard somebody speak the way she did.

"What's yours?" he asked. "I'd like to know really. So I have something to call you while you're at it." He felt his lap. He was so conceited and this was the worst part about him. You couldn't do anything about it either. So please don't hold it against him.

"You have some nerve, young man!" She kept saying young man like that meant something to him. "It won't be tolerated!"

"Oh, phooey," he said. "I was hoping it would." He sighed heavily. "Some other time, I suppose." He got up to his feet, smiling violently, and then did something very bad. He spit on the floor. It was very stupid to do because he had to clean it with his washrag anyway.

"For God's sake!" she said. She really was so angry. "Find a rag to clean that up immediately and when you're finished, you can explain this behavior to Miss Penny!" Miss Penny's the head nurse at Macauley. She's a very kind lady. I never did mind talking with her. And so it made no good sense, her saying that.

"Missus Penny! She's a great woman. She's got a sense of humor at least. However did she hire you?" Ansel would not let it drop. He never let anything drop. "You really do have a nice mouth. It's a goddamn shame you don't use it for anything. Isn't it a goddamn shame, Jack?"

"Won't you cut it out already? Is that too much trouble?" I asked him. He stared at me, fazed it seemed that I didn't play this game beside him. And then he laughed at me.

"Have I told you how funny you are?" he said. "You really are funny. You are so goddamn funny."

"About twice before you have," I said.

"Was there a special reason I did? I can't remember."

"I don't know, Ansel. I'm just asking you to stop being crude. Won't you stop?" He sighed like I'd made a very taxing request.

"Fine. I have to look for my washrag anyway. Somebody spit on the floor!" So he went into the bathroom.

"I'm sorry, you shouldn't take him very serious," I said to the orderly.

"I know much better than to do that, thank you," she said. She said that very quick and that's how you knew she was annoyed. Adults can be so very interesting because they're annoyed quite easy. I was only trying to be nice, though. I wish she knew that. "I should report you to Miss Penny for impropriety also."

"You'd have no reason to," I said, laughing sort of.

"For shoes on the hardwood, young man." I looked down at her feet to notice her wearing shoes too.

"But you have them on."

"Because I am older than you," she said. I didn't know what that had to do with wearing your shoes while inside but I didn't feel at all like having a whole argument about it either. I knew that would only drive her into something crazier. And adults have very little, ugly minds anyway. It happens when you grow up. I just hope you and I can escape it somehow.

Ansel came from the bathroom with his washrag and cleaned the spit up. The orderly said there would be another check in twenty minutes but I never saw her again. I don't know what happened to her really. She must have quit or something right after.

But anyway, Ansel cleaned the spit up.

"It's snowing still," I said to him once he got done. I'd gone over to the window to look out it again. It really was snowing still. And it was nice the way it came down too, I remember, like a dream almost. I was thinking about everybody at school and how they probably had the day at home to sleep.

"And what about that, Jack?" Ansel said. He was being funny.

"Do you want to go outside now? I have a coat you could borrow."

"Aren't you just the nicest kid around!" he said.

"Don't worry about it."

"Oh, but I'd already planned on that. Bought a string tie to do my worrying in even."

"You haven't got money."

"You're right. Oh goddamn it, you're right!"

I was glad to let Ansel borrow my coat because I never wore it anyway. He seemed glad about it too. I remember this often because I miss Ansel a lot. I really do. But he told me not to go after him, and so I didn't. Sometimes people have to go and it can be very simple if you'd like it to.

When Ansel put my coat on, I thought about Ben. I'm starting to realize in my writing just how alike they are. I'm certain that you've noticed this too, whether that was right now or some time yesterday. I don't know, it's really not so important. I had many days where I could have noticed this but I only am now. And it so very frightens me. I'd like very much to know about my world burning and how long that goes for. The next time a fireplace ash lands directly on your shoulder, do not quickly brush it away. Do a tally in your head about how long it's there for. It won't be very long anyway. Someone is certain to mention it to you, and when they do, watch them quickly brush it away. I'm telling you this because you never learn about it anywhere. And you can't go around town asking just anybody either or they might put you away.

Anyway, Ansel and I went outside. It was cold. I don't remember how cold it was, though, really. I just remember it snowing and it was quite magical. I would have liked to dance in it, but I was too nervous. I like dancing sometimes but it's sort of about who you're with, really. You could dance with somebody who doesn't know what they're doing and ruin your whole evening. Besides, Ansel was too worried about pneumonia anyways.

"I just lost my goddamn toe!" he said. I laughed at him.

"No, you didn't," I said.

"How do you know?"

"Because there'd be a lot more crying from you."

"I'm tough," he said. "I had frostbite once before and told nobody about it. I can't bend my left pinky because of it." I looked at him.

"Are you really serious?" I asked. Ansel was a very hard person to believe about anything. It really drove me crazy sometimes.

"I am, look!" He held his left hand up like he was taking a lousy oath and put down every finger but his pinky finger. So I did the very same.

"I don't necessarily believe you," I told him.

"I promise," he said, holding his pinky finger out in the way you do when you're making a promise. He was smiling madly. I just stared at him, contemplating and all. I really did have trouble believing him, but that was mostly his doing anyway. When I first met Ansel, he wore these glasses and told me he was blind in both his eyes. I don't know how that whole idea got into his mind but he was pretty good at making you think it was real honestly. He let this go on for about a week, until I walked in the bathroom one morning and saw him masturbating to this photograph without them on. I felt bad for walking in, and so I asked him if he needed his glasses and he said he wasn't blind really. I didn't believe anything he'd say after that.

I really didn't like Ansel very much at first. It's funny thinking about that now, and too bad.

He picked up my hand. He didn't let me think about it even. He never let you think about anything. I didn't pull back, though. He had these very warm hands and it was cold out.

He tried joining his pinky finger to mine but really couldn't seem to do it. And I felt sort of terrible. So I gave him this stare, and asked him again.

"Are you really serious?"

He kept smiling like a madman would.

"What reason have I got to lie today?" he said. "It's too cold out for that!"

"It really is," I said. "We should have worn gloves."

"How about tomorrow?" he asked. "And we can have drinking chocolate."

"Do they have drinking chocolate?"

"Oh yes, they just hide it in the cupboards! You have to look around for it."

So anyway, I believed Ansel about the frostbite he got in his left pinky finger. He only made promises with his right one the whole time I knew him, and that was a long while. I just don't think he could lied for that long because he would have forgotten about it eventually. Or he was the best goddamn actor I ever met, I don't know.

It was quiet once we came inside because that girl who sat on the stairs and often sang had caught a bad cold and died. It was very sad because she was younger than Ansel and me, and kids don't know anything about the world. I just hope she died in her sleep like how my mom did. It's a lot easier for them that way, I think. You don't have to say goodbye or anything. You just go to sleep, exhausted and dream. Wake up in your childhood bedroom and your dog is happy to see you of course. It could be spring there. And you have time enough. You're alright, breathe already.

So that girl's room was vacant. I think it's important you know that. I saw her parents when they came by and got her clothes and they looked just terrible. You knew the mom was crying because her eyes were all red and worn. And the dad was quiet and had that very gloomy looking face dads have when they're sad. I call it the black sky.

Ansel was running his hands under the hot faucet water. You saw the steam coming up from it, it was so hot. I was standing in the bathroom doorway watching him do this.

"You shouldn't do that," I said. "It doesn't help the cold any. It only makes it burn worse."

"Is that right? Who told you that?" he asked. My mom did, but I told him it's common sense really. "I don't think I've heard that before. Are you making it up?"

"Doesn't it hurt you?" I asked him.

"No, honestly. It's relaxing. Loosens my hands up," he said.

"But it really is no good for you, Ansel." I felt like my dad saying this to him. I mean I felt too grown, and I hated feeling that way so I went out into the room and started taking my coat off. I had a lot on my mind. I was thinking about that girl who died and her parents. I knew I shouldn't have but I can't stop my mind from anything. I got sort of mad at her parents, to be honest, because I never saw them until they came by and got her clothes. It bothered me very much, them doing that. I came close to crying even, but I decided I wouldn't do that while taking my coat off and all. It didn't seem very appropriate. And it had nothing to do with me, really. I don't know if you should cry about things that have nothing to do with you. I was just feeling awfully small.

So I did my best stopping that. I went over to where the broken spin top was still on the floor, picked it up and put it inside my pocket. I forgot I did this, though, until the other day. And I've outgrown those clothes since. How could I have done that? I gave them to this little boy down the street. I don't know what he did about the broken pieces, if he found them inside my pocket and put them back together, or laughed simply—and tossed them.

I noticed after this, the yellow taxi cab in the window again, but now it was leaving. And I could hear Ansel pissing from the bathroom too.

"Can't you close the door?" I asked him. He never closed the door when he was taking a piss. And he'd never flush the toilet bowl down either. He was a terrible roommate, really.

"I'm not a stranger!" he said. When he was finished, he didn't flush of course. And he came out from the bathroom and started pacing around. He was making the floor creak with this and so I couldn't concentrate on anything.

"Is that so necessary?" I asked him.

"Sorry, was I bothering you?" He went and sat on his bed.

"You don't have to keep wearing that inside, you know," I said. He had my coat on still and this annoyed me somewhat. I've never liked it when people wear their coats inside. You look goddamn stupid doing that. And I think it's sort of improper, too, because you make it seem like you won't be staying for very long. I just wish people would stop that.

"Have I got to take it off this very second?" he asked all innocent. I couldn't stand this, him asking that way. I don't know why. I was just feeling so hysterical. So I apologized and told him perhaps he could keep my coat if he wanted to.

"I only need one, really," I said.

"How about that!" He was all excited, I remember. "Thanks so much, Jack."

"Don't worry about it," I said. "Would you mind if I opened the window, though?" I was in great, desperate need right that very minute of some outside air that I couldn't have waited for him to answer. I was over at the window instantly, clawing practically at the frame.

It opened just barely that you couldn't put your hand out through it.

"That's so nobody jumps out," Ansel said. "Only window that opens all the way is the one in the drawing room, but they don't ever let you. I think they must hate fresh air or something." I kept trying to get it open completely though anyway.

"Why do you want it open so bad anyway?" he asked. "We just came from out there."

I was too busy listening to the window pane splitting to give him a proper enough answer. You could hear it split like, well, very much like wood does and this sound only grew louder until I got the window open.

I breathed in the cold air like you would the spring and closed my eyes. I was half mad, holding the window pane so tightly like I was a ship's captain and this was my boat wheel.

When I heard the wood split again, the window came flying down onto my fingers.

I didn't react how you'd likely expect. Its cruelty would have surprised me a year earlier, yes, but now it was just too bad timing. I laughed about it instead. Life is a very funny, so horrible thing.

"Are you alright!" Ansel said. "Really, are you alright? You should go down to Miss Penny. She could put a bandage on you."

I didn't feel at all like talking to him anymore, so I just nodded and went out into the hallway. My knuckles were hurting awful and a little bloody too. I really could use a bandage, I decided. So I started making my way to Miss Penny's room.

I walked against the wall, my shoulder lightly skimming it every once in a long while, until the janitor sweeping saw and told me to stop. I've got to wipe these walls when you do that, he said. I apologized and very quietly kept walking.

When I got there, to Miss Penny's room, I could hear talking from inside so I didn't walk right in. I think it's bad mannered to do that anyway. So I tapped on the glass to the door with my palm instead, since I couldn't make out a fist well enough to knock. You would've thought I'd broken every finger in my goddamn hands really, the way I was acting.

I saw someone approach the glass rather abruptly. I knew instantly it wasn't Miss Penny because she's not very slim around the waist, and so she doesn't move nearly that quick. Actually, I was thinking I recognized this glass silhouette from a shadow I'd once known quite well. I used to memorize shadows, you know.

Only if the sun was out, though. I really had no time in doing that when it was terrible weather.

I began to wonder in through a sort of strange, familiar maze at the possibility deeming from the glass silhouette. I thought certainly I was being misled and it was a dirty, random ploy by the electric light sculpted in long conversation with my own mind. I had never trusted a glass silhouette before. Have you ever?

I backed away from the door, so I wouldn't look too eager. I heard the doorknob turn slightly at first, considering perhaps what ordinary danger was out there in the hall, and then I heard it turn the whole way. And then the door opened the whole way. And then I goddamn near fainted because fate's a curious thing really. For there's nothing you can do to stop it. You must accept its complexity and find some brand new way to incorporate it alongside your everyday chores. You have to do them anyway.

It was a long time since I last saw Maisie Kenton, and so she looked nothing like I remembered. She had finally cut her hair short. I was surprised because she always talked about cutting it, but never would go to the hairdresser. Although it was somewhat disheveled, I thought she looked nice this way and I have to admit, I forgot just how nice looking Maisie Kenton was until that moment. Her lips still had that thing about them that I can't seem to describe because I don't quite know what that thing is. She just has these very pretty lips. And so in the fluorescent overglow, the cut she had on them was very easily noticed. I hadn't known yet what this cut was about, and while mostly uncertain, I could sense something just terrible outside had gone on. I began to worry.

"Oh, there you are," Maisie said. It was full of wonder, her voice still, and tuned so carefully it was a dream. "I've had no one to help me carry my bags. I had to carry them up the front stairs alone—you're doing that odd thing, Jack." I was looking at her—staring really—in the most violent, hazy manner I've ever had. I blinked twice even, hoping maybe just this one single time I was truly mad and Maisie Kenton was not standing in Miss Penny's doorway. But I was wrong of course. Often I am.

"You're so odd. I've missed you, you know. Now could you help with my bags?"

"Where are they?" I asked.

"I set them over by the heater. I hoped they would've caught fire already, but nothing's really in my favor lately. Is it true they have a weekly card game night? I saw it on the little calendar on the way in."

"Yes, they do sometimes. But I don't join in," I said.

"I knew you wouldn't. I saw it and thought, you know, I bet Jack doesn't do that. I bet that he doesn't! He's too good for a silly card game night."

"You weren't thinking that."

"I really was! You find some way into my head a hundred times an hour with these tiny meaning things. It's a real wonder they've only just now brought me here. I should've come with you to begin. I really am sorry about that."

"Oh, no. You didn't have to do that."

"I have worried about you, Jack—I've worried almost to death about you."

"You didn't have to do that."

"And I thought many times about calling you, but— oh, I don't know anyway!" Maisie began to cry. I never saw her cry before. She wasn't sobbing or anything. She was just sort of crying a little and you might have thought she only had powder in her eye she was doing it so prettily. But it'd be a terrible thing if somebody was crying and you just watched them because they looked prettily.

"I think I've broken my knuckles," I said suddenly. "What do you think?" I put my hands out for her to look at. I knew this would stop her from crying because she loved me too much. I don't think she'd ever admit that, though. Maisie Kenton's far too busy for admitting things. You've got to break your knuckles for the girl instead, and hope you're good and important enough to stop her from crying more.

"Jack, oh, they're bleeding! How did you do this?"

"I had the window fall on me."

"You had it fall on you?" she asked in that jokingly demeanor I'd missed wildly—and so the crying was over. "Is that some arrangement you have?"

"How'd you know that?"

"I just know you too well," she said, smiling of course, but in a newer way. It wasn't bright or delirious anymore, although it still had its many appealing colors. Red, blue and green and some blue again. But it seemed she'd forgotten those colors were even there. I saw them, though, in daylight and from a great distance—and it was the saddest thing I ever saw while at Macauley. "You can come in, you know. I've got sticking plaster in my shower bag."

"How exciting," I said, walking into Miss Penny's office. I hardly remember anything about it except how warm she'd keep it. Bitter outside cold didn't matter anyhow, she kept it warm far into the spring too. And the reason, I remember, was found eventually in the most random, worrying case of a possible winter storm.

Maisie had several bags with her, and over there by Miss Penny's heater, she was looking all through them.

"I mostly brought just my clothes," she said. "Some books, too, of course, and about three pairs of winter boots. I never go anyplace now without them. You probably won't believe this, but it's awfully cold out lately."

"I've noticed that, actually," I said.

"Oh, have you? I'm so glad. I really worried it was only me."

Maisie found her shower bag and with it the sticking plaster.

"Do you want to sit down?" she asked, sitting down on the window ledge that creaked when she did. She began unraveling the sticking plaster. "You're making me nervous with your swaying."

"Am I swaying?" I asked. I hadn't noticed this even.

"You are and you're terrible at it," she said.

So I stopped swaying and sat down beside her on the window ledge instead. Maisie had this porch swing at her house we used to sit in just about every day when it got around the perfect time for the sun to be setting. Even when it was cold, we'd sit out there with a coat put over our legs. I swear you saw the sunset best from that porch swing. It used to be my favorite thing in all of the world.

"Do you remember that?" I asked.

"Do you think I've just forgotten you?" she said, raising her head from the sticking plaster and looking at me so gently. "Take my word, Jack. It's not so easy."

"Nothing's easy," I said, putting a smile out there.

"Right, nothing's easy. You damn sweet optimist boy. Can I have your hand?" I gave her my hand and she held it all nicely like I was some tiny, brittle thing. It was lovely.

"Would you mind now if I asked you something?" I said, in the way I used to, on the porch swing.

"You just have, and don't say that you haven't." She loved saying that if you ever gave her the opportunity to, so I'd string my words specially when I could. She'd nod after anyway.

"Did you ever read the book I gave you?" I'd given her James and the Giant Peach for her birthday the year before.

"I did. I had a wonderful time reading it, thank you. Is that too tight?"

"No, that's just fine," I said, although it was sort of tight. "Do you like the color purple still?"

"Mostly. And you light blue?"

"Mostly. How's school?"

"School's boring," she said. "Beautifully boring."

"Could it be worse?" I asked.

"Probably not, thank you for asking." She gestured for me to give her my other hand so I did.

"Beautifully boring, did you come up with that?"

"On my own just now."

"It's a nice saying really." I leant my head against the window and then immediately regretted it. I forgot how the cold makes windows just terrible to lean against. But I played it casual anyway.

"I'm glad you enjoyed it."

"I did, honestly. You should write poetry sometime."
She laughed at that. I hoped she would. You've got to
hear her laugh and then you'd know what I mean.

"How's that?"

"It's just fine," I said again, turning my hands over in
my hands. "Thanks, Maisie."

She put the sticking plaster away, back into her
shower bag. And then she leant her head against the
window too.

"How do you go about your days?" she asked me. I
was looking at her, she was looking out the window,
but I was looking at her and I saw this great sadness in
her expression, one you'd only find in museum
paintings, that was never there before that day. And
that just stayed.

"I don't know really," I told her. "I haven't thought
about it all that much. I just hang around, honestly."
Maisie sighed. She doesn't like having nothing to do.
"But they've got a drawing room, and that card game
night. And you're allowed to go outside when you'd
like."

"Is there television?" she asked.

"Yes but they only have the news. Sometimes they
put a movie on, but that's only sometimes."

"It all sounds terrific," she said.

"It's just grand, better than anything."

"That's high acclaim, Jack." She looked at me—or maybe peered is the more fitting word. She peered at me, yes—better, and smiled. "Are you positive?"

"I don't believe I've lied about anything ever, have I?" I asked, only joking of course. It really felt like conversation did on the porch swing. I'm realizing how much I miss that goddamn swing just writing you about it.

"Oh you definitely have," she said, laughing very much about it. "But you're so good at telling lies I forgive you every time."

Sitting up from against the window, she kissed me simply.

It wasn't the first time we'd ever kissed, hardly that. We've kissed quite a lot, actually. It's just something we'd do if we ever got bored. So I often found it this great pleasure, really, to get so beautifully bored.

I kissed her right back of course. I remember feeling my lips awfully rough that day, though, because of the cold. And I would have put something on them before, but I didn't really anticipate kissing somebody that day. Especially not Maisie Kenton again. So I just sat there, lips all coarse, kissing her, and thought nothing more about tragedy for the second time that day.

Only, we didn't kiss for too long because, and this is terrible to admit so openly, but I don't know how to breathe properly when you're kissing. And so I had to breathe.

I told her sorry while pulling away. I really did feel bad because I like kissing her. It's just mostly that kissing isn't like swimming and so you shouldn't believe anyone who's told you that.

"That's alright," she said. "I don't know that we should have anyway." She seemed busy all of a sudden, looking around the room for anything to do. "I have to settle in. Do you know what time it is?"

"I don't know exactly. I could go and look for you," I said.

"That's alright. Just seems it's getting to be late out is all."

"It's only afternoon."

"Right. I don't know what I'm on about." She got up from the window so quickly that it creaked just barely when she did. "Is there a bathroom around I could use?"

"Maisie, and tell me honestly, are you alright?" I asked. "You're seeming really nervous." She really was.

"I'm perfectly alright. I'd just like to find a bathroom."

"There's one down the hallway on the right side they keep pretty clean. I could walk you there."

"That's fine, you don't have to," she told me. I got up from the window ledge anyway, and I'm glad I did because that's when I noticed she was kind of crying again. I just stared at her in thought for a moment, seeming to realize I don't know anything about girls except that they never tell you anything honestly.

"Who gave you that cut?" I decided I'd ask, pointing at my own lip for demonstration.

"It's just from the cold," she said almost immediately. She's great at excuses, really, you'd have to give her that. But she was glaring at me, and that glare often gave the whole game away.

"No, it's not," I said, sounding all grown when I did. I really hated it.

"Please don't worry about me, Jack. I didn't ask you to."

"Sorry, Maisie, really—but I've got nothing else to do."

She just smiled about halfway.

"You care about everything too much," she said.

"What's the trouble in that?" I asked.

"Do you leave room for yourself?" She was speaking very quiet now like the snow outside. It frightened me only because she never spoke that quietly.

"I don't know what you mean," I said honestly.

"When's the last time you ever did something for just yourself?"

"I don't know—" I went all through my mind looking anywhere for a simple enough answer, and beside the dreamy state in between the now yellowing memory, I found a good day I had alone once.

It was the day I first heard "Songbird" by Fleetwood Mac and it was a cloudy day, I remember. You know those days when the sky's got that whitish gray to it and you think it just might rain but it doesn't. It cools down instead and you can take a walk to the park where nobody's around. So that's exactly what I did.

Only a few days had come about since my mom told me she was sick, but it feels like some twenty light years when you give way to the sadness of everything. And once you do that, you've just got to wait it out. But remember in your waiting not to breathe all things deeply. That's something you'd regret eventually. I know I did anyway.

My mom had just given me the "Rumours" album on cassette and I hadn't found enough time to listen until that day. I came downstairs and saw my mom asleep on the recliner chair. My dad left a sticky notepad on the icebox saying he'd gone to the grocery store.

Sitting on the carpet, I watched my mom breathing asleep for a short while and thought about all the kinds of flowers there are. And how really similar humans are to flowers because they're so beautiful just breathing and how life's poisoning and how you lose everything steadily once you're a certain age.

I decided I needed to just empty my head. It's not an easy thing of course, it's probably a worse custom than learning to first walk. So I drank some water and put on these long, white and green striped socks I'd gotten from my grandma for Christmas. She only ever gives me socks now that I think about it, but that's alright. I don't really ask for anything too particular anyway.

I had put the cassette in my nightstand drawer that June day, thinking it'd become something I find way later on and pine terribly about for never listening. Strange how I once thought you decided your own pity feeling.

I looked around in the drawer for the Walkman stereo my mom had given me too. It had attracted some little dust already that would have glanced so appealing if I hadn't drawn the curtains earlier. I wiped it against my hands clean and opened it to put the cassette in. It's very simple putting a cassette tape in, you've just got to make certain it's facing the right way when you do.

I put the headphones on and closed the screen door kindly so to not wake my mom. I laced my shoes on the front porch steps and while stirring about in my mind everything from tiny grass hilltops to the big sky, I outlined a nail on the fourth step with just my pretty eye. And I'd tell you about how once I got both my shoes tied, I sat there for a while and did nothing but sit there for a while, but I don't think you'd enjoy it all that much.

Anyway, I ended up taking a walk over to the park. I listened to "Rumours" the whole way but I was worrying far too much about the most inconstantly rough sidewalks to really appreciate it. It wasn't until I sat down on a swing and rested my head against the chain that I grew curious about this piano I was hearing. It sounded very much almost like I knew it before. So I began to just cry, unknowing even that those piano notes would one day become the only souvenir I'd get.

Once the song finished, it was totally quiet except the humming noise from the tape just spinning around waiting to be turned over. I sat there and allowed its spinning for some time, letting the world adjust to a new world, and then I turned it over, got up and walked myself home.

I told Maisie all about this. And felt so terrible all about it, too. I don't know why I feel so terrible always. I really don't. Could be that I have the greatest day and pull it apart just for the broken glass, or could be that I'm quite mad. I don't like thinking about it too much.

Maisie just stared at me kind of sadly and said nothing and that was alright because I was already feeling terrible enough. So terrible enough that I kissed Maisie again, harder than before. And that's when I realized I only seem to kiss Maisie when I feel terrible. I spent the whole kiss realizing that that I didn't notice the floor had creaked once even.

I jumped embarrassingly and almost broke my neck turning around the way I did when Miss Penny's voice came out from pretty much nowhere.

"Where do you know one another from?" she asked, standing there in the doorway—smiling just awfully. You'd think it was the funniest thing ever, really, by how much she was smiling.

"I'm sorry—" I went to go and say, but Miss Penny stopped me before I could explain anything.

"I just wanted to know, that's all. You don't have to apologize." She walked from the doorway over to her desk, the floor creaking easy with every step she had to get there. Something about Miss Penny I sort of always found funny was she's never really quick about anything. You could be bleeding out all over the bed linen while she's taking short and difficult time up the stairs like only a water cup has spilled. "Your room's put together, Maisie. I just have to find the—" she bent over behind her desk, making her sentences come apart into these little fragments of madness. I was hearing static on the television box. "—and you have a lovely view of the stables and the fountain. Did I mention to you the fountain?"

I looked at Maisie while Miss Penny talked all in a mess, demonstrating little obvious activity. Although she didn't seem sad or anything too completely absent, my feeling that she did was of course inevitable. Next time when you look at somebody and think they're all sad at heart—move closer and realize you don't quite know them well enough to draw such a dark sky thing. You should feel a whole lot better once you do, but if you don't, what you must do instead is forget about all this and suffer full-scale every morning about those already dead and those already dying.

"The fountain doesn't work anymore but it's a nice—oh I've got it here!" Miss Penny said.

Straightening up, she had a toilet paper roll in hand like a kid would a five dollar bill they found outside a department store. On my first day at Macauley, she gave me one too. It's not the low priced kind, and they only give you it once anyway, so I take it's supposed to be some welcoming present. You have only the low priced kind they've got in the bathrooms once you run out, so it's a nice thought.

She leant forward and gave it to Maisie. "Jack—hey, why don't I have you walk Maisie up to her room? Does that sound alright?" Miss Penny asked. Her eyes moved around from Maisie to me and she did that about twice over again, so I nodded, glad to anyway.

"If it's not too much trouble, I could," I said.

"Thank you a lot, Jack. I've put her in Allie's old room, do you know where that is?" Allie was the little girl who died that I told you about earlier, the one who'd sit on the stairs and sing. So I knew exactly where that was.

"Isn't it right by the staircase?"

She started to reorganize her desk it seemed. "I'm behind on a lot of my filing so, really, thank you, Jack. It was nice meeting you, Maisie. And if you ever need anything or would like someone to talk with, of course, you know where to find me at." I told you she's this nice lady and all.

I got Maisie's bags and showed her to the room. It wasn't too far from Miss Penny's office, if I'm remembering it all correctly. Her office was close by the staircase—so yes, that would have to be right.

"Was it hot to you in there?" Maisie asked.

"It's that way all the time," I told her. "I really don't know what it's about either."

"It's the winter storms probably," she said. "People worry about them more than you'd ever think. I'm sorry for kissing you, by the way. I don't know that I should have."

Having a girl apologize for kissing you is really the worst thing you can experience if you're a boy and especially if you like that girl. Do your greatest in avoiding it and cry only when you get alone. Don't use all of your time, though. You come to find there really are better things to do. Like reading a poem and letting the sound of voices flatten just enough to kill you.

"I wish you'd stop that," I said. We came to the most abrupt stop halfway up the staircase. There was a short pause in promising troubled conversation, until Maisie tapped again on the thin glass, and downhill the long stream went. I lowered myself in.

"Stop what, Jack?" she asked.

"I don't know," I said. "I mean you're just always saying how you're sorry when you kiss me, when I really don't mind it all that much."

Maisie stared only at first, so I just did the same. I almost got around to worrying but then she broke out into a kind of smile that made you forget about every stupid thing. So that's what I did.

"You're so brand new," she said. "I'd barely recognize you if I didn't know your voice."

"I could say the very same about you."

"Oh, I'm not brand new, Jack." I hated the way she said this because it was too thinly and too real like she'd grown up seven whole years in just the previous few months. And there was nothing more I could do about it. You can't do anything when you're away too long.

"We can't be standing here all day," she said, looking away from me. So we started back up the staircase.

Maisie's room was much nicer than mine and Ansel's room. It was painted beige, though that seemed to be slowly dying away into a boring white color again. She had a rocking chair placed nicely in the corner right beside the window that indicated sitting and reading letters in, or sunbathing in, or losing your whole mind in. I never thought Maisie would find suitable use for it, but she did plenty enough. And she told me all about it when we'd play Go Fish in the common room, and I realized she was entirely remade. It'd taken me quite a while, but when I did, I accepted the passing disappearance like you do getting somewhat older and never got over it.

The ceiling light fixture was just replaced, it seemed, because there was new paint closing it in. I worried how she'd keep cool if she stayed through the summer months because she no longer had a ceiling fan like Ansel and I did. I was silly to do that, though, of course. She would hardly be staying two months.

Maisie did not have a dresser, but instead a whole brilliant closet with enough room for two people to stand inside at once.

"It's just brilliant, Jack, don't you think so?" she asked when we both had settled and fit comfortably in. I was sort of jealous, I'd have to admit. Ansel and I only had dresser cabinets. I'd never admit that directly, though. I'm not that green eyed anyway.

"Absolutely brilliant," I said. Dangling before my face was the string attached to the lightbulb—yes, she had a lightbulb in there even—so I pulled it down.

"I'm so glad you did that. I'd almost forgotten what you looked like," she said. We both laughed. I get farther into this story and realize how funny it is. Oh, but not really. Maybe the cleverness of her has bewildered me too greatly.

Now that I had her attention, and there was hardly a threat to be had of Miss Penny coming in, I thought I'd finally ask Maisie about the subject of her being there at Macauley. All color was gone from her face when I did, like a terribly sad old ghost, and I thought maybe I shouldn't have asked, but it would have come up in time eventually, and greeted me resentfully. So I couldn't wait any longer.

"Oh," she just said at first, looking away from me again at some damn pretend thing. "It's a long story. I thought you'd have figured it all out by now."

"I've never once figured you out," I told her.

"Just don't make it some big deal, Jack, please," she asked politely offbeat of me. "Everyone's doing that already and it's not anything that's so worrying—" She was talking awfully quick now. I could barely keep pace.

"Maisie, could you look at me?" Her eyes were still half-pivoting the goddamn air.

"It's not all that exciting, either, on top of everything that's happened, so I don't know why you ask."

"Could you look at me for God's sake!" I said kind of too loudly perhaps. She looked abruptly at me in a pleasantly betraying way—her eyes almost glass entirely, and laughed. "It's not funny," I told her.

"Did someone tell you that it was?" she recoiled, smiling in her poor attempt.

"You just laughed."

"Because I've never known you to raise your voice that way. It's very cute."

"Oh, shut up," I said, rolling my eyes probably. She was always making you roll your eyes in some way.

"It's true! I could never be afraid of you." We looked at each other how we'd always do, nice and gently, pushing aside gray clouds and those curtains that hang so menacing and heavy. It was all that'd ever matter, really. "You do make me nervous, though, Jack. From all your talking so much."

She gave me that certain look only girls can give you, and then she breathed in deeply like she had the most important thing ever to say. And then she repeated sentences I could have written my own, and might already have. I believed her, though, anyway.

So it was Christmastime when this happened. You need to know that because the roads get so icy in Christmastime—don't they?

"It was my fault," Maisie admitted to begin. It didn't seem very hard for her to say that, so she must have really meant it. "I just want you to know that first, Jack."

"Okay," I said, nodding also. She went on.

"Everything seemed to just go quiet after Ben, but you out of everyone probably don't have to be told that," she said. I hadn't heard his name mentioned out loud in a while, so it was kind of funny, actually. I don't mean that to be terrible or anything. I'd just almost gotten to thinking maybe Ben was this whole great joke I'd made to keep busy myself. It was nice to know he wasn't another dream I once had.

Ben was the best person I ever knew really, yet it's strange when I write about him. I could spend days on his memory, laying out the prettiest words you ever read. But if I had to read it all back from the start, I'd just feel so very dishonest. Because you can't make the world change. And while it's the most terrible thing, you get used to it eventually. I promise that you really do.

But anyway. For this part of the story, you need to know that Ben was the best friend I ever had, and that he died on September 27th, 1986. I don't need you knowing any more about that for right now. It was only a few weeks since my mom died, so I don't like thinking too much about it or I just get so sad. It's that simple enough honestly and so I hope you can understand. I'd really appreciate you doing that. You adjust your glasses when they're too big, the same way you do your clothes, often your ghosts, and a brand new world.

I found myself at Macauley a week after Ben's death. It was my dad who brought me there, and the afternoon he did I hated him the most I ever have. And the next month or so I stayed feeling that way about him, until one night, kept up by Ansel's snoring and this reoccurring dread, I realized my dad's all that I've got now. And so I reassumed my position, cross-legged, and got over myself. Sometimes you just have to get over yourself. You can either do that or go mad. It's your decision really.

Maisie told me that my dad came by her house that same week.

"He just let me know you were alright," she said. "Everyone was so worried about you, you know."

"Sounds nonsense," I said. "Probably not everyone."

"No, I mean that. Everyone. I had people I never met coming up to me at school asking about you."

"Were you honest with them?"

A short silence came about.

"No, I wasn't," she said.

"Why not?" I asked.

"Because what was I supposed to say anyway, Jack?" she asked. "I was a terrible friend who thought—"

"I don't think you were a terrible friend."

"You wouldn't. Because you're so nice it's awful, Jack."

"Would you like me not to be?"

"Stop. Stop that. Do you get what I mean?" I laughed. She hit me lightly on my shoulder. "Stop!"

"If I was this nice to anybody who wasn't you, they'd be crazy for me. Do you know that? Absolutely crazy."

"You're right, but not in the way you're thinking. Now do me a favor and stop talking."

Maisie said she told everybody at school I went to stay with my grandma for some time. I was really kind of glad she did that because I didn't want them thinking I was this madman. People talk, and once they do, it's almost impossible getting them to stop. It's amazing, honestly.

Everybody seemed to move on, Maisie described. I knew that would happen anyway. You could break your arm on the new park swing however many times you'd like to—people go to work, make their living and entertain. Streetlamps, you'd find on most nights, turn on all the same.

But not Maisie Kenton. Maisie's absolutely hated Cradock since forever, though not for the faulty sidewalks or the absent color in the weather like how I do. But rather for all the hearts that beat all the wrong ways.

"It killed me every day not knowing how you were, Jack. I should have written you, or come and visited you. I owed you the simplest things."

You could hear her voice shaking with sorry regret, the way voices do when they're asking you to give out another chance. I would forgive her, of course, I mean I already had. I'd never blame somebody for the very thought of owing me the simplest things.

"It was sometime in the afternoon, I don't quite remember exactly when," she said. "And I was driving down Felix from Eisner's with a bag of marbles I'd just gotten for Michael." Michael is Maisie's little brother. "I was at a red traffic light when the bag tipped over in the front seat, and the marbles went just absolutely everywhere," she said. "I tried reaching over to pick up a few since I was stopped anyway, and I'm thinking my foot must have come off the brake pedal because the next thing I knew, the car was rolling forward and I'm driving into the lamppost on the street corner there. And you know how the roads get when it's cold, Jack. Right? They get so icy, and you can't stop your car quick enough."

I found her asking me this somewhat odd because, it seemed, really, that she was telling me about it instead. Had she wanted me to believe the road had become so wet through the cold that you'd find yourself accidentally driving into a lamppost? Because I could hardly ever believe that. I did, however, run it through in my head anyway, because it was something to do. And then in a manner close enough to the one she'd put on, I responded fittingly.

"No, I don't," I said.

Maisie sighed a certainly practiced sigh.

"Oh, well," she said. "They're particularly bad this year. Just covered in ice all over—just all over." She was always a lousy liar, and I'd gotten to know this by the simple way she'd repeat her words. People repeat themselves accordingly.

"What street corner?" I asked.

"I was coming from Felix," she said, employing her hands in presentation a little too much.

"I think I know where you're talking about," I told her. But I didn't. Because there's no lamppost coming from Felix anyway. So I decided I'd just leave it alone, and let it play about in my mind. What dangerous thing a thought can be. "Did Michael ever get his marbles at least?"

"He didn't," she said, smiling completely in a way she never had before. It frightened me a little, honestly. You would have thought she gone mad. "And I had this cardboard giftbox I was going to put them in, but I lost most of them anyway, so I never bothered about collecting the rest. Would you have, Jack?"

I looked at her, almost prompted to by the confused exchange, and smiled too.

"No," I said, shaking my head unusually regular at the concern. "I don't know that I would."

Chapter 5:

You're Not a Madman, You're Just Born in Manhattan

"Once I drowned in the rain," I said. "Another time I got pulled into a swimming pool by nothing. I saw everybody above. Even my mom was there."

I was talking to Ansel. We were folding little paper airplanes in the drawing room—well, I was folding them because he couldn't fold for anything. I was always having to help him out. But I didn't mind anyway.

"How was your mom there?" he asked. "I thought you said she was dead." You really couldn't be mad at him for saying things how they were because that's just how Ansel was. I'd gotten used to it.

"In my dreams she's not," I told him.

"What you said doesn't sound much like a dream. I mean goddamn, Jack, you're talking about drowning. I don't think you ever hear yourself."

"Oh, leave me alone and don't start."

"I won't, I won't," he said.

I gave him his paper airplane creased neatly in just the right way so it'd catch a gentle wind stream. I really am good at that. If you wanted, I could probably make you one sometime. And we could go out flying them together after. I know all the places to catch a gentle wind stream.

Earlier today when I saw Phoebe, she asked me about my nightmares. I didn't feel much like talking about it, though. It was something I noticed on the way there that was cause for my terrible disinterest. I stopped my bike at first because I almost ran into this girl who wasn't paying very good attention. She had the prettiest red hair I've ever seen, and I really mean that. You'd probably think so too if you saw her. Or maybe you wouldn't. I forget I don't know you all that much.

But anyway, it was when I stopped my bike that I realized the songbirds were still quiet. Did you notice? And then I began to wonder if they were always so quiet for this many days. I can't remember when I last heard one sing.

I got very depressed realizing that, and I must have had on a sad face or something because that girl I just told you about started asking me things you'd only ask somebody who has a sad look about them. It scared me almost.

"I'm sorry. I didn't see you coming," she said. "Though you really shouldn't have your bike on the sidewalk anyways. It's good I noticed in time before you ran me down." I could hear her talking just fine but my mind was all over the place. I'd have to find the songbirds another day. When I'm not already so busy.

"I saw you there," I said, looking at her, noticing first her green eyes. I couldn't believe it! I'd only ever known one other person to have green eyes and that was Ansel. His were a little darker than hers, though, I'd have to say. "I wouldn't have hit you."

"I'm certain that you wouldn't have," she said. I could tell she was only joking around, and it was strange almost because normally you can't ever tell that about somebody when you've just met them. "Are you late for something? You're in an awful hurry."

"I'm not. Why do you ask anyway?" I said.

"I was just making conversation. Do you know what that is?"

I had nothing clever to say, and you only have so long to come up with something when talking to a girl if you want them to think you're pretty sharp witted. Otherwise they find out too much about you.

So I just laughed. She looked surprised I did that.

"I must have missed the joke," she said—all serious about it too. I got a little worried because I didn't want her to think I was making fun of her or anything stupid girls think boys do.

"Oh, I was just—" I was stumbling all through my words now, steadily too, worst I ever have like small boys sometimes do. I like playing it cool when I can, but I couldn't seem to today.

I expected her to cut in and maybe put a great end to my terrible nervousness, but she never did. She just gazed at me instead like how girls do when you're acting so foolish. With those slightly dim closed eyes.

I'm all too familiar with that gaze. Maisie used to give me it just about every day I'd see her.

"Finish your sentence through," she finally said. "I'm not in an awful hurry."

"I just thought you were teasing me when you asked if I knew what conversation was," I said. She was really staring me down. "I mean, yeah, I know what that is. I'm not so stupid."

She just kept staring at me. It was driving me crazy. I've never liked it when people stay looking at you for so long. Sometimes I find myself staring at somebody who's pretty but I always look away when I'm caught. I don't want them thinking I'm goddamn mad. But this girl didn't seem concerned all that much. I felt almost like she'd found some way into my mind and was reading about my life's work. Drawing lines over lines.

And then she just smiled in this very big way. I never saw someone smile so big. I didn't really know how to feel about it. She did have a nice smile, though.

"I was teasing you!" she said while smiling still. "Ease up some. Would you do that? You look very dreadful. Are you dreadful?" Now she was looking oddly at me like maybe she felt sorry for me. And the strangest part about it was she really did look sorry. So for that reason I didn't mind it all that much.

"No, I'm fine," I told her. "Why do you think that anyway?" I just read that back and got worried—I hope

I wasn't sounding mean. I really wasn't trying to be that way or anything. I was only asking.

"Let's drop it," she said—that sorry look absolutely gone. She had just a regular one about her now. I've really got to work on my goddamn tone delivery. "You and I both have somewhere to be anyway."

"That's too bad. I was just about to tell you all of my troubles. Every last one I've got," I said. She laughed at that. I was awfully glad she did, too, so I could relax a little. I can never relax knowing I upset a girl somehow.

"Oh, I'm flattered. But, really, I have somewhere I have to be. If only you'd told me before when I first asked. Now you'll have to wait until the next time." She was pretty amusing.

"Where do you have to be?" I asked. She didn't answer me at first, though. She was busy looking all through this bag she had that I had to ask again.

"I'm meeting somebody, if that's alright." She really was looking in every part of her bag. "Don't you have a date too?"

"What makes you think that?"

"Your awful hurry," she said, looking up at me. She was smiling in that very big way I wrote you about earlier, and putting her hand out. She was holding five dollars. For me, presumably.

"What's that for?" I asked.

She nodded her head toward my bike.

"The air's almost all gone from your tire," she said. I glanced down and it really was going flat! It was good she mentioned it. I don't think I would have noticed otherwise. "I wouldn't want you hitting anybody because of it, so that's for you. Five should be enough. I have a bike too." She tried to give me the five dollars again but I wouldn't take it. I don't like handouts. Does anybody?

"I'm not taking that," I told her. "And you don't have to do that anyway. I can just walk myself home."

"So you don't have a date?"

"I never said that I did."

"That's my bad, you're right. You didn't."

"Why'd you think so, may I ask?"

"You'll have to wait until the next time," she said again, smiling. I really can't describe her smile another way that's not just the word big. I know I've used that word a lot, but it's only right. She put the five dollars back in her bag. "I'm glad to have met you. Now I know to watch out for bikes."

"I wouldn't have hit you," I said, laughing while I did.

"But we have no way of knowing."

"Not until the next time anyway." I was pleased by how quickly that came out. I told you I could often play it cool.

"I knew you'd understand. Now I really do have to go, but you take it easy," she said. And then she just walked off. It all happened so fast I'm realizing I never even asked her name. I'm really so terrible at asking names. You can't take it too personal or anything. I hope she didn't. I'll ask the next time if I can remember to anyway.

I pushed my bike the whole rest of the way to Phoebe's office. It was probably best I did that anyway because the sidewalks really get rough when you near Paton Street. You want to be careful so you don't go flying onto your chin. I got thrown from my bike once and it hurt so goddamn much that I cried so much and my eyes went all blurry. I'd never wish that feeling on anybody, except maybe Westley Reid. Although it's possible he's not felt anything in his life anyway. Some people just don't feel anything. It's almost extraordinary. I'd find myself pitying them if I didn't already find so many other things worth pitying.

Have you noticed what they've done to Paton Street? Oh—sorry again, I forget you might not live in Cradock. My mind's become all the same. They've shortened the tree branches over the road a page or two. I noticed this today when I noticed the rosemary air was dying away—why do all good things die away—and when I saw the new sunlight about the foxglove Phoebe has. It used to be placed just right on the windowsill where the only sunlight came in. But now there was plenty going around. Enough to make your head spin, yes, but not to start you completely over again.

"My bike got a flat tire. I'm sorry," I told Phoebe when I saw her. "How late am I?

"You're not very late," she said. "How are you feeling today?"

"I'm alright," I said. She really doesn't know what goes on in my mind, but I decided I wouldn't give her trouble like how I did last week. I only just saw her last week if you aren't keeping up any. "Except now I've got a flat tire. I had to walk all the way here from Felix."

"Do you come through Felix often to get here?" she asked.

"Oh—only sometimes." I had a feeling she wouldn't like my real answer so I ended up not being honest. I always come through Felix to get there anyway because I have my best memory down that street. I wouldn't mind telling you about it. I'd like to have it written into a long poem so I don't ever forget. I just don't feel like writing about it today because then I'd get all sad and I don't want to feel that way currently. I certainly didn't feel like talking about it either so I moved the conversation along. "I'm writing a lot."

"Is that right?" she asked all gladly. I've really come to notice how adults ask you things all gladly. My mom used to do it too so I'm not complaining about it necessarily. It can be nice having someone speak that way to you. And it almost makes you think adults pay great attention, but only they don't, because they've grown—in my experience at least. But I don't know, maybe paying attention isn't worth that much anyway. My mom was the only adult I ever knew who really listened—so maybe it does absolutely nothing but kill you slowly on the most ordinary morning.

I sat down on Phoebe's couch. I almost sighed until I remembered where I was. You can't just sigh in Phoebe's company or you get in some trouble. She starts asking you things.

Phoebe came and sat down in this other chair she's got. I'd like to sit in it sometimes but she mostly does and I won't take that from her. I feel odd enough sitting on the couch already. Lonesome, really. I don't even know why. I'm realizing I feel that way all the time. I must quit that. But it's better than nothing.

"What are you writing about?" she asked.

"It's hard to just categorize. I write about wherever my mind goes that day," I said.

"Where do you find your mind normally goes?"

"I don't know. It's different places each time."

"Do you want to talk about that?"

I sort of wanted to, honestly. Because you don't ever get an escape, and silence won't come if you don't prop the window open wide enough.

"We could," I said. "If you want to."

"I'm asking you, Jack, if that's what you'd like to talk about today. I won't make you." She didn't mean that in a cruel way or anything—I don't know anybody very cruel—she just meant it very straightly. Sometimes I appreciate Phoebe talking that way. It keeps me wide awake.

"Fine, yes. I'd like to talk about it," I told her.

By now I had closed my eyes. She kept talking to me the whole time while I amused the prettiest daydream. I moved to some great city they forgot about me in. I bumped somebody's shoulder on Jones Street and smiled because they didn't recognize me. I was a stranger who only got sad one day in September, and my dad called in the morning time.

I had one afternoon in New York City a few years ago. I was barely ten so I can only put so many details together at once. If you ever want to understand the world better just close your eyes, so you don't attract unnecessary light. Draw behind the second story closed blinds, warm yourself in excitable delight or something. I haven't got any more rhymes.

My aunt just had a baby and so we were on our way to visit her in goddamn Vermont. We made a stop and had soft pretzels in the park. There was a man playing on the saxophone those bright and stunning notes of that song "You're Not A Madman, You're Just Born in Manhattan." My parents danced closely in a circle and they did no harm.

Of all the afternoons I've ever had, that one's probably my favorite. I almost wish that you were there—a member of the dancing crowd preferably—and not just reading about it. I'm not very good at telling stories how they really were. But it doesn't matter all that much anyway. I just want them told.

"Where's your mind at today, Jack?" Phoebe asked. I opened my eyes now, leaving behind the well-furnished brown study. I would have to find some way back. I'd arranged the furniture too carefully.

I looked at her. She really was letting her hair grow out, I noticed. It was longer now than my mom's ever was. But what relevancy? I can see through nothing and see my mom in it too.

The girl I saw on the way there was also floating in the current of my head. I felt the pressure a few yards out from my brain. But I wouldn't dare mention anything about that. I worry Phoebe would never understand, and I work much better alone anyway.

"Right now I'm thinking about how my bike has a flat tire," I said. It wasn't completely dishonest because it was on my mind somewhat. But it wasn't a very concerning thought. I don't even have those anymore.

"How much does that worry you?"

"Not a lot. My dad can probably fix it anyway."

I haven't lost a bag of marbles over it just yet, I wanted to say, but Maisie wasn't there and that would leave only you and I knowing what I mean. And you weren't quite there either.

"Is your dad at work today?" she asked.

"He didn't mention having anywhere else to be." My dad is always working and it's not a very big deal but of course Phoebe thinks I have some bad feeling toward it. I really don't, though, because my dad is not a bad man. He's just very busy and forgets about the time so often you might think I hate him. But it's like I told you. He's all I've got.

"Did he leave before you?"

"I think he did—yes, he did. It was about an hour or so, if I have the time correct. He had to work at three something."

"What was your conversation about today?"

"How ever am I supposed to remember that?" I said. "I don't keep notes on conversations I have. I'm not anything like you."

"Don't be so forward, Jack. We've talked about that."

"I was just honest! Should I not be honest?"

"Oh, stop that already, won't you?" she said. I didn't mean to be troublesome, really, only honest, and so I did stop. I didn't want to upset her or anything more. I just get bored having the same conversations. I'm certain you would too.

"Fine. Do you want to know what I wrote most recently about?" I asked, hoping to redirect the conversation away someplace better. And it did so in about two seconds. It's very easy distracting somebody. You've just got to ask them something instead. Put them out to sea and let the curiosity sit with them so directly. It works for me anyway.

"Yes, I would. Do you mind if I take notes?" She didn't really give me time to answer, though. She was over at her desk to get her clipboard and settled back in her chair before I even detailed a thought. People never wait for you.

Phoebe was just looking at me now, and I knew enough by that look that she waited probably for some kind of honesty. But no one was around that I owed honesty and I'd far removed myself from the forest fire burning in the name of honesty. It's flickering lit cool orange, your city, and people love dancing over it because you let them. It's really the most terrible habit you have. You've got to stop that even if it takes all of your body's strength. You can rest when you get finished anyway.

"I had the wildest dream," I told Phoebe. "And then I had it again the very next night. It was awfully bright-colored. I can remember everything about it."

I've had these very detailed dreams ever since I was a kid. So detailed you'd believe they're fixed or something. But I promise they aren't. If I'm sincere in anything it's dreams. I have so many that I'd find no use in making them up. I just want you to know I wasn't telling Phoebe a lie necessarily.

"Do you feel like talking about it?" she asked. She's always coming off so nice that I feel bad about the whole memory thing. But it seemed to me worth doing once. I had people to save.

"I just don't know what to do about them, my dreams," I said.

"Why is it you have to do something about them?" she asked.

"Because isn't that what I'm supposed to be doing anyway? Shouldn't I have forgotten my mom by now?"

Phoebe at that moment was looking at me and I was looking at her, too, I think for the same reasons. I knew I had made the mistake of being too honest. I felt really so awful. My dreams just get me so down sometimes.

"You don't have to forget your mom, Jack. Do you really believe that?"

"I don't know," I said. But I did know plenty enough. I just didn't feel like saying more about it really. I'd already let it go so very far. I don't know how conversations get away from me. I have to forget about my mom someday if I ever want to do anything easily again. I cannot get dressed without making it a chore. "Now can I say my dream?"

She looked hesitantly at first. You would've thought she didn't want to hear it that much anymore, but only because you don't quite know her enough. Don't forget she's too goddamn nice and that maybe I abuse her listening.

"Well alright—yes, go ahead." She gave out a smile and a beautiful green light hue.

I go back to June.

Once I've caught my own breath, I realize, somehow, winter has come up right behind me. Does this happen when you close your eyes to dream too? I feel my mind shivering. Could it be a head cold? I wander close towards the Macauley madhouse, but in my dreams I never go inside. I let myself have the ordinary feeling I've gone to war instead.

I twist around in this lonely red booth. My fingers trace the leather peeling off. I never could sit quietly anyway.

I set about my ordinary wonderment. My conscious harmony streamlet. Who had painted the doorway red? And why that color red? Don't you like red anyway? Look at the black and white tiling instead. Listen to the popular jazz song overhead—you're not a madman, you're just born in Manhattan.

I look at my mom. Even in my dreams she's put together still, and pretty like the early morning time blue. She has this great smile on, too, just like you saw often in magazines. It was the kindest thing you'd ever know and it'd make its appearance on every strange occasion like some gold lame shoe. Remember it most in the car radio and how it broke, so she sang all the way home.

"I remember when you were a boy," my mom said. "And how you would—oh, you'd spend so much time outside, Jack. I'd have dinner made ready and your dad and I, we'd try and have you come inside, but you'd never want to. Do you know we'd have to pry you from the tree branch right outside? You just wouldn't let go. And there was this one day when I had to—your dad, he was at work, and so I had to carry you in alone. You were just so mad. You hated me for many days after that. You would only talk to your dad for everything."

"I don't remember that," I said. "Sorry I acted that way."

"Don't be. I don't mean to upset you."

And there in the noisy fluorescent light I saw this mousy flicker in her eye—the very same one she had when my grandad died. Someone had opened the upstairs window and outside there was a quiet riverbank along the once repaired tile. Put on your finest garments and look down below. Hold on steady, or jump out.

"I know you don't," I said. I really believed her about that. I always believed her about anything. Don't you with your mom? "But are you alright? You look like you're about to start crying."

"Oh, I don't know. It's not easy to explain, Jack." And so she did begin to cry. But not how you'd think. She didn't sob. Instead it was something more quiet. "It's just not very fair to you that I keep it a secret."

"Keep what a secret?" I asked. I could feel my heartbeat so very forceful that it gave me a headache. It was a terrible feeling.

"I only just found out—" she said in this voice that you don't hear often. Not that you'd want to anyway.

"Found out what?" But I knew. I knew just by looking at her.

I felt the ordinary course of everything. And it's worse than sharp blades cutting.

"I don't mean to upset you," she said again. Her voice repeated throughout the dream. I couldn't hear the song that was on anymore. She was wiping her face with her hand. I offered her a napkin, and every napkin after that, but that wasn't enough to stop the rough water outgoing.

My mom begins to scream at this exact moment in the dream. It goes all throughout the Redgold Creamery setting so ear piercing. Every window gets smashed in and the doorway swings open like a very fast plane has gone by.

At first I cannot recognize why she's screaming so terribly, but then I notice the singed water streaking onto her face. Her crying was burning her face.

I realize my dream is recurving memory. I wake up so no one gets hurt further.

I told Phoebe that whole thing and how every night it's the same dream. How I wake to this sound of rain when it's not raining. And how I know the paperboy went missing. But I don't know whether she got any of that. She was looking too confused.

"How often do you dream, Jack?" she asked. I watched her tap her pencil on her clipboard, and tap it again, and tap it again in between these short pauses. It was annoying me somewhat. I wished the pencil would just break into pieces leaving it unfixable, and then I felt sorry for wishing that.

"About every night," I said.

"And that's all you dream?"

"Every night—sorry, could you stop that?" I pointed at her pencil. "It's distracting."

"Oh, my fault. I hadn't noticed." She set the pencil down. "You haven't spoken much before about that day you had with your mom. I think it would be good if you told me about it, or at most, what you remember from it, Jack."

I thought what a dangerous idea that might be! I'd said too much already and still that wasn't enough.

I counted in my mind every scenario that could play out wrongly if I told Phoebe about that June day and the colors I saw. How this girl's arm fixed up in a red sling was darkening steadily gray. And the doorway among that too. Phoebe would think I'm goddamn mad still! Most people don't know anything about colors anyway. How they come and go and you can't do anything about it. You just can't.

I finished counting and decided, without speaking, to stand up and walk over to the window. In the window's glare, I thought I saw my mom's face. But I knew I hadn't anyway. I just had the same eyes.

I looked out at the quiet street, moving like dust on a shelf. My eyes raised to the tree covering that once created a sort of playful gallery almost. Now it was dull.

"Have they cut the branches?" I asked. "You almost have a full view of the sky now."

"Yes, I think they have," she said. "Do you want to sit back down?"

"In just a minute. I remember now."

"What do you remember?"

I held my breath. What to do? I could be honest, I thought—my mind is so very often suffocating anyways. I could be different and new and just agree with everybody about everything. But there's someone I'd betray in doing that. And those green eyes roam already in the corner enough.

I was quiet for too long. Phoebe broke onto the boxcar of thoughts. She's always doing that in some way.

"Jack?" she said. "What do you remember?"

I sighed. I'd have to do this or she'd never stop asking about it. So I pulled myself together.

"My mom had wanted to go out for ice cream. I thought nothing about it, except only that it was a hot day and we'd go out for ice cream on hot days," I said, looking out the window still. I paid close attention to the course of breeze and how it moved so doubtfully that I missed the storm clouds altogether. I miss the important things. I dream the wrong dreams.

Out through the window, I saw everything about that June day, but nothing yet wrong. My dad had gone into work early—or so I thought anyway. I don't know. Could I have observed so poorly the facet tracing on simple reasoning? Could I be so young? I thought for a moment if I put my head through the window, maybe I could have June again. I promise now I'd listen. Describe it in lovely remarking. I've grown older now. I really have. And I know everything. I really do.

We sat down in the same booth I mentioned from my dream, and once we did, my mom set a light pink cassette tape on the table and slid it across to me.

"What's that?" I asked. I didn't know what it had meant, although it captivated me forever. It had a man and elegant woman on it and only they appeared in black and white. He had his one leg up on a footstool, with this strange chain down on his beltline. She, in toe dancing shoes, had her leg draped over his knee. On it read: Fleetwood Mac/Rumours

"It's my favorite," she said. "I don't know how I forgot I had it. I found it in a box under my bed, and my first thought was how you'd enjoy it."

"Do you mean it's mine?"

"It's yours. I have a stereo at home that you can use it for too."

My mom was a very sentimental woman. If she didn't want something anymore it promised certain trouble. I've never known that to be wrong, and so I knew everything was wrong.

I looked into my mom's eyes now heavily watered down.

"I'm going to die," my mom said. I almost didn't recognize her voice.

My fingers trace over again the leather and I give time for change—if I only could. Really, I didn't say anything. Instead I laughed somewhat. I've regretted that ever since. But what do you do when you lose your footing?

I looked away from the window at Phoebe. She wasn't looking at me. She was busy taking notes.

"I'm sorry," I said. "It's a bad story really."

"Don't be sorry, Jack," Phoebe said. "I think it's a fine story that you told very well. Was there more to it?"

I thought about it for a short while, fingertips retracing memory the way they did the leather, and came to nothing more. I told Phoebe everything about that June day. I was honest for the first time in some time, and I can't believe I'm admitting this, but it made me feel better. I know that seems stupid.

"No, that's it. Did you expect more?"

"No—I just wanted to be sure." She stopped writing and looked at me. She was smiling too, mostly. She has this sort of strange, awkward smile where you never know if she's really smiling purposely or not. I don't mean that impolitely or anything because it's just the way it is. "I'm glad we're having this talk, Jack. Are you?"

"I am," I said. "I really am." I left the window alone and sat down again. "Can I ask you something? If you don't mind."

"You can ask me anything you'd like," she said. She really is a nice lady.

"Do you feel happy?" I asked. I was just curious, really. I've never asked anybody that because I don't care too much. But there is something gorgeous about today.

"Well—yes, I do feel happy, Jack." She sounded relieved almost like maybe she was scared about what I might ask. I didn't mean to get her panicked. "Is there a special reason you ask?"

I said no because there really wasn't. "What time is it now?"

"You don't have to go if you don't want to yet, Jack. I won't send you away."

"Oh, I know, but it's not that anyway. I have to get home."

Phoebe stared at me.

"That's fine," she said. "Let me drive you."

I was about to remind her that I had my bike, but I'd completely forgotten about my flat tire! I have to get that fixed sometime tomorrow.

"You don't have to do that," I told her. "It's not very far and it hasn't gotten dark either. I can just walk."

"Are you positive? I won't mind."

"Yes, but thank you for offering anyway." At that moment I got up and walked over to the door, and then came Phoebe's voice one more time, so I looked back to her.

"Jack—remember to keep writing." I nodded, well, yes. "And if you want to come with your journal next week, we can look over it together."

I sighed, but not to where she'd pick up on it or anything. I did that because I just wasn't that interested in her reading my journal. She'd really think I was goddamn mad and I really mean that. If she knew about you, I'd probably never write you again, and I'd hate that. How would I spend my time otherwise? So that's the trouble happening.

I smiled eventually, though, and nodded my head politely again to avoid the madhouse door held wide open. You have to memorize the stoplight pattern to keep from it. But I've told you that before—haven't I.

"I'll see you next week," I said. Opening the door, I was welcomed by the rosemary fallen behind trying to explain its place in the neighborhood still. I was feeling more sorry they cut the branches outside. But you'll find your way home in some time again, I thought.

I felt this strange relief on my way home, now that I wasn't wearing that heavy pinned ribbon any longer. But still there, in the back of my mind, drifted the very thought of everything. I worry I may never feel, among many other things, complete warmth again. I have left the second floor window open for too long, and now I'm left fastening some blame on a stranger's blouse, so being that it doesn't belong to me.

Before I went home, though, I decided I'd walk over to the Norman Bauer bridge, just to take a look. And so that's what I did. I put my elbows on the rail and my chin to rest on top. I looked at the river and gave thought to the very thought of everything. Life spent floating could be so wonderful a life, if only they'd let you do that anyway.

I remember rumors circulating when Norman jumped that he had very bad head trauma from the rocks below the water. I'd almost believe that if Ben and I hadn't ever jumped the bridge before. It's really not that high of a jump, and there aren't rocks underneath to cushion you. The water's deep enough for you to come up just fine. But first you'd have to want to. Maybe Norman just didn't want to. Maybe the water was lukewarm and so he decided to stay.

I also heard he had a leech up his nose when they found him.

I tapped my finger on my elbow and watched the water beneath. It goes so fast, I felt almost like a whole hour went by just standing there. I kept still so I could focus on just hearing the water move but there were people around and their voices tore little holes through what quiet I had. It really bothered me so much, though I wish it didn't, that I decided I'd leave altogether. I got my bike and walked home.

My dad wasn't there yet when I did get back home, so I put my clock radio on, but he should be any minute now. I just want to say again that I love my dad. I really do. Sometimes I'm awful to him for nothing. I wish I could stop that because it's like I told you already, he's all I've got now.

Earlier, just before I wrote you, I was sitting on the floor in deep thought about the redheaded girl I almost ran into on the way to see Phoebe. I was doing that and you really wouldn't believe what song came on my clock radio! I almost couldn't believe it myself.

You're not a madman, you're just born in Manhattan
Every time you let it happen
You let it happen again
I wish you'd stay
And wander off toward a better place
Find your best dressing case
So you could stay

And wander off toward a better place

<u>Chapter 6</u>:

Right Before the World Closed In, Shutting the Door
Behind It

I'm starting back at school tomorrow. Phoebe and
my dad seem to think it'd do some good for me since
I haven't gone in a long time. It's almost a year now
since I last went, and just so much has happened since
that I don't know how to feel about it.

Recently again I've started missing Ben. And I know
being at school will only make that feeling worsen. I
thought about telling Phoebe this, but I just couldn't
figure out how. I didn't want her thinking I'm a terrible
person feeling that way either.

If I asked my mom about this, she'd tell me I'm not
terrible, but that I'm too good of a kid, actually, and
my heart's just like fine China because it breaks so
easily—and that's what it's for!—she'd say—that's what
it's for, just so you know.

But I can't ask her anything of course. Anything ever
again. I don't know why that's so hard to understand.
I'm really trying. But is that enough anymore? It's
starting to hurt very much thinking about. I just miss
her a lot.

I miss them both.

Anyway, you wouldn't know this, but I haven't
written in some time. When I last wrote you, I was

listening to a favorite song of mine, and I closed my eyes and I opened them again to cry. I don't know why I did that because the song doesn't sound that sad anyway, but I couldn't stop or anything. My dad came home, and he found me in my room just crying. He sat with me for a while and then brought me a water glass. I really appreciated it.

"What are you listening to?" my dad asked. He was talking about my clock radio, and the song playing. "Oh, I recognize this one. This one's a great one."

I smiled at him. My dad, I noticed, looked kind of sad, though. Sometimes I forget he's missing my mom too. I just find that so interesting, how we can feel the same thing. I wish I could drown the feeling in the water below the Norman Bauer bridge forever. It would mean those nearby just standing around laughing wouldn't have anything to laugh about anymore. While I'd have plenty.

Phoebe never read my journal, just so you know. I just keep acting like I forget it every time I get there. I don't know how much longer I can keep that up, though, before she realizes I'm doing that knowingly. She's not so stupid. But I haven't had another nightmare since I wrote you previously, so I don't know if that's really so important anyway. I haven't dreamt for the whole month of August. You might find that sad, but I find the sleep more beautiful.

So I was thinking earlier about Ben, and how I never went back to school after that September weekend. It's going to be so different there without him because I've never had a first day of school that he wasn't there for. I really mean that, too. I met Ben on my first day of kindergarten in Miss Seavey's class. She sat him next to me, so in some way she was the best teacher I ever had, really.

Last year when my mom was in the hospital, she asked me and Ben to take a lot of photographs on the first day and so that's what we did. I feel sorry, though, because I don't have that many photos of Ben anymore. If we ever got to taking pictures and printing them out, Ben always wanted to keep them, and of course I'd let him. But I really wish I hadn't now. Maisie told me his parents moved away a couple of weeks after he died, and so they probably have them in a box in their new attic wherever they went off to. I'm not upset at them for leaving or anything. I know why they had to go. I just don't want to ever forget him.

I could probably write about my best memory now. I just had to give it some thought first, and find the right wording and set it right, too, because it's too lovely of something to do wrong. It was a great day, I mean, and the scene was so illuminating that if I shut my eyes today, I feel everything about it still.

But anyway. Ben and I had spent the whole day at the creek in just our boxer shorts and had you flowed downstream starting from the Norman Bauer bridge, you could have too. Although Norman hadn't jumped yet then, so it was just a bridge, unexciting and wooden, like most bridges are anyway.

Ben was throwing stones directly at the water. I was watching his shoulder—unclothed, and his seemingly unrelaxed posture when I realized he'd started looking different. I told him I could show him to skip a stone as you're supposed to, but he got displeased at my offering.

"I know how to skip a goddamn rock!" he said. You could hear the defeat in his voice. Accompanying by was the water subtle and fluent in its course. I bent down and let it run through my hands so I could wash off the dirt I had in my fingernails. I don't remember how it got there.

"It doesn't look that way," I said. He looked back at me, shaking his head and smiling in this easily affected way. You'd have to smile too.

"You wise guy!" he said, diving toward me. He knocked me back completely into the water, punching my shoulder awfully gentle while doing so. I kneed him in the gut, just barely, but enough to bring him down. I knew how to playfight reasonably well. In my effort, I was able to get on top of him, and something about that felt spectacularly good.

"If you wanted a kiss that bad you could have just asked. I would give you one!" he told me.

"I bet that you would!" I said, letting him go, stupidly, then. Employing his new freedom, he splashed the creek water up into my eyes. "Are you crazy! You've pissed in this water!"

"It's a free flowing river, Jack! It won't kill you or anything."

"You don't know that!"

"Oh, don't give me that line. I know everything!" He laughed. Writing that out now, I realize he said that in the same way Ansel would. Really they would've gotten on well so nicely. And we could've gone to the creek together and spent the whole day there, too, sitting opposite of absolutely nothing ever. I would have really liked that.

But it was never the same at the creek once Ben started dating Marigold. I don't mean that I had some hard feeling or anything really because I'd invite Maisie sometimes too, but Ben invited Marigold to the creek and to the arcade and to everywhere. And the absence of just his company felt cruel in some way that I can't explain because I haven't figured it out yet, still.

Anyway, Ben felt around under the water for another stone. Once he found one fit enough, he tossed it to me.

"Since you're just so desperate to show off," he said, smiling at me.

"Oh, well, it's in your wrist, and yours is way out," I told him. "You have to flick it just right so it spins. You want it to spin so it skips."

I held the stone in between my thumb and index finger like how you do when you're about to skip one—I mean I do hope you know how to skip a stone. I flicked my wrist and let the stone fly off against the water. I counted about four times that it bounced!

"Didn't know you were so good at that," Ansel said.

"But I thought you knew everything?" I asked. He laughed, and if only you ever heard him laugh, you'd compare it to the darling sound songbirds whistling have.

I don't really know how this happened next or anything because I was facing away from Ben, looking for my stone in the water, when it did. It was just awfully good timing—the new stone he'd found leaving from between his hand at the very moment I bent down to retrieve mine own. So when I looked back at Ben, instead of his stone countering the water, it hit me right in the mouth, above my lip.

I didn't realize how much blood there was until I looked down at my stomach coated in it. It was hurrying down from my mouth like the river water does the standpipe at the Norman Bauer bridge. Really, it was that much and going that quick. And so there I was, paralyzed, bleeding out into the creek, poisoning the tap water ingredient they don't filter out.

"Oh shit!" Ben said. I didn't know him to swear that way before.

I said nothing because I knew it would hurt so badly if I did anyway, also because I didn't want any blood going inside my mouth either. It tastes so horrible, don't you know that?

And then I fainted from the whole spectacle, or that's what Ben said I did anyway. I don't remember much about that part except waking up to Ben kissing me, trying to wake me thoughtfully. I'd only ever kissed Maisie before that and I've only gone beyond that thought one time, and so I don't know if I should again today because it's not very easy writing about.

My eyes sort of danced, signing myself back to everything I could have just left behind. Ben noticed right away of course. He was up too close not to. I saw everything about him in that moment, noticing that in his eyes, glaring at me, there was some worried storm gone off to sea, indistinguishable from the real thing. He looked just how he did when I broke my arm on the park swing all those years ago. His bottom lip wouldn't stop trembling like it were a cold morning and there was my blood recent on it too. I felt awful about that and I could have resented myself a whole lifetime, but I was distracted by never having someone that close before instead.

"I seriously thought you died, Jack!" he said. I remember feeling his words breathe out on my skin he was so close, and they felt warm and reminiscent of the best afternoon.

"Did you really?" I asked through my suffering. I was glad to know I still had some clever ability even when I'm bleeding, but I don't think Ben was. He seemed upset instead.

"You weren't breathing!" he said. His voice was shaking loud enough to fill an empty space—a million empty spaces, honestly, and it would sit there forever. "For a whole minute you weren't breathing! I didn't know what to do! I thought I'd have to leave you and go find somebody to help—"

"I can breathe alright now," I interrupted telling him, hoping he could recover with this detail somehow.

"Because I had to kiss you that's why!"

"You didn't have to necessarily. You must have wanted to."

He looked at me like he had something important to say that was pressing on his mind, possibly harming the fabric paper by not doing so. And then he looked like he'd completely forgotten what. Sometimes I think Ben did this on purpose to distract you and just make you wonder. But anyway, he just laughed after. I don't know at what, and I never did find out that day either. He just said, "What a menace you are, Jack Boyd. You had better drink some water," and he went over to the green sunlit exterior where I'd set down my bag that had my water bottle in it. He got it for me, and my cloth towel too.

"How do you feel?" he asked, coming back through the water to where I relaxed. And curiously enough, I felt that way, too. Relaxed, I mean. I was bleeding out, while also feeling the best I ever had in the weeks since my mom died.

He gave me the water bottle and towel—oh but before he did, he twisted open the bottle's top for me. I just thought that was nice of him to do.

"I feel alright," I told him. I had some discomfort, yes, from my lip split open, but really I did feel alright otherwise.

"I'm glad to hear that," he said. His smile brightened somewhat, and so did the sunlight colored grandeur that came down through the tree branches. "I'm sorry I don't know how that happened. I wasn't taking aim at you, I swear. You were right that I don't know how to skip a rock. I feel horrible, Jack. I mean look at how much you're bleeding!"

I put the towel, coincidentally beige and for that reason, apparent, up to my mouth. When I brought it down to see, it had lots of blood dampened into it, and I could taste the blood now that tasted so awful.

"It's not so much blood," I said, although it was, and I probably should have gone to a real doctor, but that's not what we did.

I drank some water, swallowing blood so dreadfully with it too, that way I could get up and make it to Felix Street where the Eisner's drugstore is. Ben helped me stay surfaced the whole way there, putting me up rough against himself. I didn't put my shirt back on and he didn't either, and he was sweating a whole lot that it got on me, but I wasn't going to make trouble over that.

"I'm going to find you some Neosporin and band aids," Ben said.

"And somewhere to wash your hands probably," I joked. He had blood on them from holding me. He laughed, but only sort of. He seemed really unsettled.

I sat and waited by, feeling so confused and alone, outside on the street curb while he went inside. I gave him the five dollar bill my dad always gave me anytime I'd leave the house, so he could buy everything necessary. He came back out with Neosporin, band aids, a Milky Way bar, and two Cokes—everything necessary. He brought a wet paper towel, too.

He sat beside me. While inside, he'd cleaned off most of the blood I'd exposed him to, but I saw some neglected in his fingernails still. I didn't mention it, though, because like I said, he was acting really unsettled. And the face peering at me that I'd known for many years looked just so empty and scared. I didn't know it yet of course, but it wouldn't be long before I saw him that way again. It would be later that night, right before the world closed in, shutting the door behind it.

"Keep looking at me," Ben asked, and so I did. I had stopped bleeding by then, but he brought the wet paper towel he had up near my mouth anyway. He began to lightly clean around it, until every spot of the remaining blood was gone. "Not letting you die on my time yet," he said, so innocent to how those words would circle my head today, just echoing resonantly.

"How does it look?" I asked.

"It's better," he said. "I don't think you need stitches." Even though looking at my scar now, I probably did. He undid the top to the Neosporin and squeezed some out onto his index finger. "Is it alright if I put some of this on now? So that way you're not left with a scar." I nodded, knowing though that the Neosporin couldn't prevent it from scarring. My cut was too deep for that now. It was some miracle, really, that he was able to hit me so hard.

He finished applying the Neosporin, and got onto opening the band aid carton he'd bought.

"Are they G.I. Joe?" I asked. It was a red box that had Flint, the character from the show, on it. I haven't watched that show in a long time, but when I did, my dad would let me stay up late on school nights to. Ben must have remembered that.

"Yes, they are," he said, showing me the box. "I thought you'd like that best." He opened it, and tearing the paper apart, placed the band aid so awkwardly above my lip. He touched it over to know it was all the way on. "Now you're brand new!"

"I couldn't have gotten there without you," I said jokingly.

"So you mean you're indebted to me," he said in the same way I did, handing over one of the Cokes he bought. I opened it myself. "I really am sorry, though. I didn't mean to hurt you."

"I know. You said that once already."

"I know, I know. I just feel so bad about it, Jack."

"I've had worse things happen lately," I told him.

"I know and that's the part I feel most bad about," he said. "I thought because of everything that we'd have a good day at the creek, just you and me, and then I let it completely fell apart."

"I'm still having a good day," I told him. He looked at me, shaking his head just as though he were questioning the certainty of that remark. "Really, I mean that. Keep shaking your head because you won't change my mind about it."

He laughed, and so I knew he felt safe again. I listened to him take a deep breath, and drank some of my Coke while I did. I remember that was hard to do with that goddamn band aid on, so I had to take it off for Westley Reid's party later that night. My cut was somewhat better by then at least, but I shouldn't have gone. I should have just let that goddamn band aid be goddamn difficult instead.

It was so quiet for a moment, and I shut my eyes to it, and listened only to Ben breathing. I contemplated the good in the world through this and decided that I could be alright forever.

I should have known that required more.

But it was so quiet for a moment.

"Could I ask you something?" Ben said, leaving behind the quiet in the corner setting alone. If I'd known about when it'd be so quiet next, I wouldn't have let him ever do that.

"You just have, and don't say that you haven't," I said. He laughed, knowing I was only making fun of how Maisie always said that anyway.

"I just have to know—have you ever like anybody? Besides Maisie, I mean, well—do you like Maisie?"

"I like Maisie of course," I told him.

"But is that it? Have you never liked anybody else?" I wish you could've heard the way he was asking me this because I don't know how to describe it, really, but for a kid in great need of having to know absolutely everything. Only now he's found himself wandering brave amongst some little known feeling and relying on his best friend to join him there.

"Are you asking for yourself?" I said—joking so terribly. I should have known I'd made some mistake in conversation when he didn't meet there in the same demeanor.

"Oh, that's alright. I was just wondering," he said just ordinarily.

He was staring closely at his Coke bottle as though some kind of distraction was there floating around in it. Maybe he thought a tiny dead fly would surface eventually, saving him out from this conversation and into one not so apparently difficult. But that wasn't going to ever happen, so instead we just sat there quiet, facing away from the honest truth that could be so easy if I'd only felt him tap on my shoulder.

We sat there for so long burning my Coke out of its sweet taste that I was glad to have finished it. I haven't drank Coke since that day, actually, because I never liked it much to begin, and Ben was the only reason I ever really drank it anyway. He could barely go a whole day without having one and I'd have to remind him just to drink some water.

"Have you noticed how people are staring?" Ben asked.

"No, I haven't," I said, looking around at Felix Street not that occupied except for some people walking slow toward nothing probably. You'd never find the streets busy in Cradock, certainly not on hotter days, and not so late in September when there's nothing much to do anyway. But for the people that were out today, yes they were staring at me and Ben. At first I couldn't understand why, and then I remember we weren't dressed that properly or anything. We had just our boxer shorts! I mentioned that to Ben.

"It could be that," he said. "I'm deciding on whether it's that or you being covered in blood. I'm thinking it's a draw."

I started to laugh.

"I don't know how I forgot about that," I said. He started laughing now, too, and so everything was fixed and easy again.

"Do you know how Marigold's leaving?" Ben asked suddenly, confusing me what this had to do with anything before. I sighed privately, knowing this conversation would drag on. He constantly found some way to get there, leaving the matter so dead looking from all of the talking he did about it.

"I don't remember you telling me that," I said— playing sarcastic of course. I knew he was upset enough about it.

He completely disregarded that I said anything.

"Is Lancaster a long way?" he asked.

"It's Pennsylvania still," I told him.

"I don't know if her mom likes me enough anyway." It was just about time for him to begin voicing every thought he had about the subject. His face was someplace, categorically, but I don't know where. "So for me to go stay with them sometime seems just impossible. She doesn't like it much when Marigold invites me out places with them. She always has this sort of bored expression—"

"I think you should stop this," I said. "It's not the worst thing in the world if she doesn't like you."

"I know it's not, sorry. I shouldn't have brought it up."

"No, it's okay that you did. I just mean that even if her mom doesn't like you for some reason you've convinced yourself about, you have Marigold, still. Don't you think that's most important?"

He looked at me like I'd said something so crazy, and maybe I had, I don't know, but I knew by his eyes, that desperate and thin glassy surface, that I'd said plenty enough. I think if I wasn't there, he would have cried.

"And it's Pennsylvania still," he said, repeating me. "So never mind all of that?"

"Right," I said, and repeating him the same, "So never mind all of that."

And so we closed that conversation off—forever, actually. We just didn't know anything about it then.

In time we had to go, because Ben said he was cold, and Westley Reid's party was nearing anyway—there we would dance alongside each other, terribly how you do among everybody moving around and in the way, but dazzling too. I felt everything and everything was so real.

I promise to write about that night someday eventually, but I only meant to write you about going back to school tomorrow. And how I'm not very excited, but feeling really nervous instead. I just wanted somebody to know that.

Chapter 7:

First Discovering the End of the Song

I saw Marigold for the first time in a very long time today, and my heart had that sinking feeling when I did because I was certain she'd hate me for something I didn't mean to do anyway.

I'd just gotten to school, and I was standing in front of my locker when she came up behind me.

"Jack Boyd," she said, talking nice. "I've wondered about you."

I turned around sort of easy to look at her because I didn't know what to expect and I didn't want to react poorly or anything. But she looks about the same, except her hair's sort of lighter now, from the summer, probably. She has this nice tan going too. And she was smiling at me.

"Marigold, hey," I said, and then, completely dismissing any sort of well thought reason, I asked, "How are you?"

I felt behind my neck go red. I'd never apologized so quickly.

"Jack, please, it's fine," she said, though I could hear the sadness in her voice. "We shouldn't avoid addressing each other normally forever. I think that's something we should agree on now. Don't you?" I forgot just how straight she could be.

"If that's what you want, of course," I told her. She nodded, smiling still.

"Do you not have a bag?" she asked. "How do you plan on carrying your books around?"

"I only have two classes. I'm doing the rest of them at home. Mrs. Bernice fixed my schedule so I could do it that way." Mrs. Bernice is my counselor, just so you know.

"So you won't be at school much? Did you want that?"

"My dad thought it would be good if I started back off slower so I don't get too ahead of myself or anything. I don't think he's wrong about that. I should still graduate in June anyway."

"Oh, well, that's nice. I'm excited to graduate."

"Are you wanting to be a nurse still?" I asked. For the whole time I've known Marigold, she's wanted to go to school for that.

"I am," she said. I was glad to know something ordinary remained throughout the many separate promises we never meant to break. And the feelings we had, too. "I haven't decided where I want to go to school yet, though, but I'm looking. Somewhere faraway, I hope." I nodded. It made sense why she'd want that. "What about you? What are you doing?"

"I'm writing some lately. I think I like doing that."

"Do you think you want to be a writer?"

"Maybe, I don't know yet."

"You don't have to decide right this moment, you have time. On the subject of that, I should be going. I have Mr. Levings first period." I laughed.

"I also have Mr. Levings first period."

"Do you really!" she exclaimed. "I don't know why I'm surprised because you were always so smart. Ben would talk so much about that. Meanwhile I never thought I'd be taking an advanced math class."

I didn't expect her to mention Ben so early in conversation. I honestly expected her to never mention him again.

I kept from the name.

"Do you want to walk there together?" I asked instead. "I mean we don't have to of course. I just thought I'd ask."

"I don't mind walking with you. I'd like that, actually."

So that's what we did. We walked together to Mr. Levings class. I looked mostly at the floor the whole time because I could feel people staring. I don't even want to know what they were thinking because there's absolutely no way it was anything good. Marigold must have noticed.

"I know you're probably nervous," she said. "People are going to stare all the same, though, Jack, and I'm sorry, but you have to get used to it."

"Do they ever ask you anything?"

"It started off that way, everyone asking what happened," she told me. "I worried they'd never let it go."

"People never let anything go apparently," I said.

"Well, they almost did, until Maisie's car accident, too."

"Oh, yeah. She told me about that."

Marigold stopped walking. And then practiced whispering.

"I don't want to be impolite when I ask you this, Jack, but were you at the Macauley place? Maisie said you went to stay at your grandma's but I didn't believe that very much."

I sighed, but I knew I wouldn't be able to keep that from Marigold too long. I mean she had it figured out anyway.

"I was there, yes," I said. "Did everyone know that?"

"No, I just thought so. Maisie can't lie very well. Have you ever noticed how she repeats herself when she does?" I laughed.

"I have noticed that!"

Marigold laughed somewhat too. I felt good about that.

"But I'm sorry you had to go there," she said. "Did you want to?"

"I mean my dad just didn't know what more to do, and it wasn't so bad."

"Maisie was there, right?" she asked. She was talking quieter than before. I didn't like that. "What did she think of it?"

"She couldn't have found it very nice if she felt it was so necessary to run off. That's what I've told myself anyway."

"She never mentioned where she was going?"

"I don't know anything about that."

"Do you think she's still alive? I just have a terrible feeling."

"Don't talk that way!" I said, inspiring some nearby glances when I did. I lowered my voice. "Sorry, Marigold. I just don't like thinking about it."

"No, I'm sorry. I shouldn't have asked you that so plainly."

"That's alright," I told her. "I mean, I woke up one day and she was just gone. I never said a proper goodbye or anything so yes, I think she's still alive. I hope she wouldn't leave without a proper goodbye."

"Oh, that's very sad," Marigold said, looking at me sad too. I would've felt some bad way about it, but it was Marigold, and so I don't think she meant anything by it.

"Are we close to Mr. Levings?" I asked. I was going to put the conversation into the most simple cardboard giftbox if I could and toss it away. "I don't want to be late or anything."

"Oh, right! I'm sorry!" she said, the warm presence in her voice happening again when she did. You wouldn't have known we just had a conversation about something so terrible. "It's just around the corner. Oh, and, you don't look that much different, by the way."

"Did you expect me to have crazy eyes?"

"I did, actually, and I thought you'd be paler. But you've still got that handsome skin." I smiled. I forgot just how kind Marigold was.

When we got to Mr. Levings' class, there was no assigned seating and so that meant we could sit beside each other. I was surprised Marigold wanted to because Casey Morris is in that class and they used to be good friends on the cheer team together. But maybe they aren't anymore, I don't know. I didn't really ask Marigold anything today. I could later today, though.

Anyway, Mr. Levings is nice. He has a boring personality and that's the greatest personality a teacher can have, honestly. I've never liked when they're too excited. It just puts me off. He must've known who I am, though he didn't mention it. I really appreciated that. I don't like attention so much anymore.

My second class was English and funnily enough, Marigold's in that same class too, so we walked there together of course. She told me about her summer and how she got her driver's license. When I told her I still haven't gotten mine, she said, "Don't. I can take you wherever you need."

It's so nice having a friend again.

Mrs. Watson is my English teacher, and she was actually my ninth grade English teacher, too. But I don't think she remembers me because when she called out attendance, I had to correct her on how to pronounce my last name. When I did that, I noticed some of my classmates moving around in their seats to look at me.

"They must get the newspaper delivered," I whispered to Marigold, who laughed. Once that class was over, though, she asked me if I ever read the newspaper headings from that weekend last year. I told her I've read them over many times.

"I'm sorry," she said. She was saying that because her dad's the editor at the Cradock Post, the only newspaper company we have, and so that meant he oversaw everything and let it get printed the way it did.

"It's not your fault anyway," I said.

"Jack, you should know I asked him not to print anything bad."

"I take it he doesn't listen very good."

"No, he doesn't, and I'm sorry."

"Really, Marigold, don't be sorry. I understand."

"I don't think you understand, Jack. I just think you forgive too easily," she said.

"Is that bad?"

"I think so, Jack, yes."

"Oh, I haven't really thought about it."

"What's that?" she asked then. I didn't even realize it, but I was scratching my arm the whole conversation. So of course that made her notice the goddamn bitemark I have there. It had faded somewhat but scratching it made it red and noticeable, apparently. "Did someone bite you?"

"In Macauley, yes, my roommate did." I think I told you before, but it was the new roommate I got when Ansel left who did that. His name was Sawyer and he was so terrible.

"That's bad, Jack. Did they give you stitches?"

"No, they said I didn't need them. They just put some kind of fabric on it to stop the bleeding and that's what it did."

She looked sullen. I never really saw Marigold look sullen.

"They should have given you stitches," she said.

"It's alright now."

"If you say that again, I won't believe you."

"Fine, sorry," I would have said but the school bell rang instead, and so that meant we both had to go.

"Are you busy later?" she asked.

"I don't think I have anything."

"I'll come by your house then. Bye, Jack." She left for her next class. She's taking cursive.

I couldn't stay at school anymore since both of my classes were over and I'd probably get in trouble for just waiting around. I didn't want that on my first day back, so I started making my way toward the front office. And you wouldn't believe it, but I saw that girl I almost hit with my bike when I did. She was facing away, over by the printing machine, but I knew it was her just from the red hair.

She was the only person in the front office when I got there.

"Excuse me," I said. "Do you know where Mr. Pane is?" Mr. Pane is the man who works behind the desk. He's old and sad and keeps the records of attendance so I have to speak to him before I can leave.

"On holiday," she said. She was facing away still but I didn't have to see her face to know she was only making a joke.

"But I just saw him this morning."

She turned around with a new stack of papers occupying her hands and attention, apparently, because she still hadn't looked at me or anything.

"He's in the bathroom," she said, looking up finally. She had that big smile on her face when she did, and then her eyes got big too. "Don't I know you!"

"I don't think so." I thought she would've forgotten about the whole bike thing. Some people just don't forget anything despite weeks going by.

"How's your flat tire?" she asked, setting the papers onto the desk, and sitting down on the spin chair Mr. Pane has.

"It's fine. My dad fixed it. How was your date?"

She laughed. I'd hoped she would, but I think she was only doing that mockingly.

"He wasn't very nice, but thank you for remembering."

"Oh, I'm sorry, I didn't mean to—"

"You're absolutely good. I shouldn't have told you I was doing that anyway. I don't know you well or anything."

"Well, I shouldn't have asked you that anyway. Really, I'm sorry."

"You shouldn't apologize too much or people won't believe you when you say it."

"Oh, right. I'm working on that."

She picked up a pen out from Mr. Pane's pen cup and started clicking it unnecessarily.

"What did you need him for?" she asked.

"I'm going home," I said.

"Already?"

"I only have two classes."

"Oh, look at you, cool guy."

"Do you know when he might come back?"

"I don't. He didn't give me every detail of his bladder trouble. If you want to just wait, you can ask him about that when he does get back. I hear he has a bag down there."

"Who told you that?"

"Nobody, but that's what happens when you get old. They replace your personal area with a plastic bag."

"I don't want to hear about that."

"Well you already have."

"You shouldn't go around telling people that."

"Oh, you're a boy. I know you've heard worse."

I almost sighed but decided I wouldn't give her the enjoyment of my defeat. So I smiled like I could all the time and her eyes met mine. I forgot they were so green. I wondered if I stared long enough, would I find Ansel leaving too?

She was clicking that pen still.

"Could you stop that?" I asked.

"Is it driving you mad?" It was, yes, but I knew if I said that she'd keep clicking probably.

"I just don't want you to get ink all over yourself or anything."

She stopped.

"Do you consider everything?" she asked, putting the pen back into the cup when she did.

"Just about."

"I hope that doesn't kill you one day." I was surprised she said that.

"That's a wild thing to say to someone you don't know well."

"Oh, that doesn't really matter. You probably needed to hear that more than anything."

Normally I would hate someone for telling me what they think I need, but I couldn't seem to do anything except smile at her. I really should get to know her better if that's going to be the case every time.

"What are you doing up here anyway?" I asked. "Do you not have a class?"

"I have a free period, so I'm an office aid. I get to print and staple and do all things I find great excitement in." She seemed pretty impassively dazed saying that.

"Is it the same every day?"

"Probably, yes, until a boy comes in dutifully reminding me of a terrible date I had."

"I said I'm sorry!"

"I know you did." She was smiling. I really like the way she does that. "I can write a note for when he gets back if you have to leave right this moment."

"Could you do that?"

"I do have a purpose, you know," she said, taking the same pen out from the cup and clicking it only once. She found a sticky notepad nearby. "What's your name?"

"Oh," I said. It hadn't really occurred to me that I'd have to give my name in someplace along playful, front office conversation and that scared me bad. But, I found the worrying stupid because nothing came from that occurrence. I mean if she knew who I was, she didn't react anyway. She just wrote my name down onto the notepad when I said it. She must not read the newspaper.

"I'll see to it he gets this note," she told me, meaning Mr. Pane.

"I really appreciate that, thank you."

"Wait, I should ask, is your mom outside?" she asked. "Or your dad, whoever's picking you up. Because you don't have to wait outside for them if they're not. It's too hot for that."

At that moment, when she said that, I really wished she'd known my name from the newspaper, so that way I wouldn't have to explain how my mom's not picking me up because she's dead. I didn't anyway, though, because I wasn't going to make the conversation so tragic. If I ever get to know her obviously I'd mention it someday.

"I rode my bike, actually," I said.

"Right, of course you did." She was smiling big. "Well, ride safely, please. I wouldn't like seeing you with a broken nose tomorrow."

"I'll pay close attention."

"I'm so glad to hear that," she said.

I smiled at her and waved very small too. I've really come to dislike saying goodbye. Even if it's very small.

Ben and I found ourselves at Eisner's a lot when the school day ended. We'd always get a Coke and sometimes a magazine, if we had enough money to. So today I thought I'd do that again.

I set my bike against the wall outside, held my breath and let it go after nine seconds, like Phoebe had me practice before. I felt uneasy still, though, but not so bothered that I couldn't go inside.

I found a magazine that had David Bowie on it, and remembered seeing the movie "Labyrinth" last summer with Ben at the Silver Colony. I never saw that movie again because it scared me so bad that I had nightmares for a whole week. But I had a nice time at the movies that night, I remember. I think I did anyway.

Marigold was busy with some cheerleading team thing and Maisie was away at her aunt's house in Washington, painting the pool house this burning red she told me lots about when we talked on the phone earlier that day. Earlier that day, too, Ben got his license and so that meant he could drive us to the movie.

"Sorry the air conditioning doesn't really work that good," Ben said.

"Oh, don't worry about it, that's alright," I told him. His parents bought him this used Sedan that had faulty air vents, but I hadn't noticed even. I was so distracted by how I'd known Ben almost my whole life and now he could drive. He must've noticed this.

"Are you good?" he asked. "You seem far off."

"I'm just thinking."

"What are you thinking about?"

"I don't know." At that point in time, I'd only known for ten days that my mom had cancer and was certainly dying. And I'd only told Ben since Maisie was away.

"You don't have to think about anything right now," he said.

"I wish it was that easy."

"It could be if you let it." Sometimes I really wished I had his mind.

"I don't think so, Ben, but thanks anyway." I looked over at him and saw his knuckles white from holding onto the steering wheel so hard. "Are you good?" I asked.

"I'm so good," he said. I could recognize the polite sarcasm in his voice, though.

"I don't think you're breathing any," I said.

"I'm breathing plenty," he swore, though I knew him better and he would exhaust conversation when he got so nervous. In the very same breath, he asked, "When does Maisie come back home again?"

"Some time next Monday."

"I bet you're excited about that."

"I don't know. I haven't told her about my mom yet."

"Oh, well, I mean that's alright. She's not going to react poorly if that's what you're thinking. She loves you too much."

"I know." I sighed. "I just hoped it would go away."

"I know," he said. And then we just sat there quiet, except for the struggled breathing noises his car vent would often make. Ben was the only person I could just sit quietly with and not feel so uncomfortable. He just had that magic about him that felt like a brief summer night as though forever.

I would have thought the moon was especially bright if I didn't know they'd just put a brand new screen in at the Silver Colony. I saw it from the ticket office.
"It's 90 feet wide," Ben told me.
"How do you know that?" I asked.
"I read about it in the paper."
"Oh, I don't ever read the paper," I said.
"I know, that's why I'm telling you about it."
He crept the car up to the ticket window and paid the clerk for two tickets. It never cost too much for a ticket there, but I didn't like knowing I owed him in any way.
"I didn't ask you to do that," I told him.
"I know," he said, looking over at me loosely good humored and determining. "Because you never ask for anything."
"I can get the snacks," I offered. I still had money to use that my dad had given me.
"If you want to," he said. "I wasn't implying that buying your ticket, though."
"I know," I said. "Because you don't ever imply anything."
He laughed.

We parked sort of close to the screen, I remember, though it didn't really matter where you parked because you saw the screen just fine anywhere.

I meant only to look around at the cars but when I did that, I saw this boy and girl kissing each other so harshly in the car beside us. I might never understand why people kiss in cars because isn't it cramped enough? I think so anyway.

I was taking off my seatbelt when Ben noticed them too.

"That's Westley and Casey!" he said. I looked back at the car again and it really was them.

"Oh, I didn't know they were dating."

"I can't believe it!" he kept saying. His mind was completely stopped by the amazement, while I didn't care all that much. Ben apparently never knew it, though I'd made it plenty obvious to pick up on, but I never liked Westley Reid, and so I certainly never cared who he was kissing.

"Are you staying behind?" I asked, opening the car door when I did. He was still looking over at them. I had to whistle at him to get his attention back.

"Sorry, I just can't believe that."

"I know, you've said that already."

"But I'll come with you. I'm not sending you alone."

"I hoped you wouldn't do that."

"I know," he said tauntingly. I smiled, and so did he, probably. I like to think he did anyway.

At the concessions we got two Cokes and a big popcorn. Ben and I would often share a popcorn because I could never finish a bag on my own. And it was just cheaper that way, too.

Ben wanted to use the bathroom before the movie started, but I didn't have to, and so I waited outside for him. I was standing there when Westley Reid and Casey Morris walked by. I hoped they wouldn't notice me, but they did of course.

Westley called out my name, incredibly noisy in doing so, even though I was only feet away from him.

"Is that Jack Boyd!" he said. "I know Jack Boyd anywhere!"

"Hey, Westley," I said back. I couldn't just disregard him. He was right in front of me now, and so awfully close that you got spit on every time he'd talk. He always stands too goddamn close and spits on you when talking. It really gets on my nerves. I hope you never meet him for that reason, and of course so many others too.

"What's a fine looking man like you doing alone?" he asked. He's really the most goddamn worst person you might ever come across.

"I'm waiting for Ben," I said. "He's just in the bathroom."

"What, did you two come together?" He practically lost himself in the amusement of that question, I remember. He just couldn't stop laughing.

"Actually, yes, we did," I said. "Ben just got his license today. Have you gotten yours back yet, Westley?" His license was suspended for hitting the stop sign by his house. He was always doing that. He would get it back that summer, though, and hit the stop sign again, because no one really cares about anything.

"I didn't know you were a smart ass, Jack Boyd," he said. I've never liked how he says my whole name when talking. And I've never known anyone else who has my name so it makes no sense doing that. But anyway, once he'd said that, he wasn't laughing anymore. He got closer to my face and you might think he'd hit me or something, but Westley Reid doesn't have the goddamn nerve. Casey must've not known that yet, though.

"Come on, Westley," she said. "You promised you'd buy me a cherry Coke."

I looked over at her and she was giving me the coldest stare, I remember. I wasn't upset or anything because I never liked Casey much either. She was mean to Maisie one time.

"Fine," Westley said. He smiled at me, properly mocking, and patted my cheek when he did. "Won't you give Ben my best?"

Casey pulled Westley away and they went off probably to get her a cherry Coke or something like she'd wanted. I don't know, I had no reason to keep up with them anyway.

Ben came from the bathroom a couple of minutes later. I didn't mention to him seeing Westley and Casey because he would've wanted to find them sometime again if I did and I just wanted that night to be me and Ben. But of course nothing's ever so easy.

We found our way back to the car, and when we got there, Westley was leaning up against it, chewing tobacco and spitting it out on the gravel in the most off-putting way.

"There you guys are! You kept me waiting!" he said.

"Westley!!!" Ben said—you'd find the exclamation points are necessary because he really was that excited. For whatever reason.

"Did he give you my best?" Westley asked Ben, looking at me when he did. "We chatted while you were taking a piss. Jack Boyd's a funny guy, did you know that?" He softened his voice close toward some quality of whispering but not enough so I couldn't hear him or anything. And I know he made certain of that. "I think he's a little gay, too."

"Wouldn't you like to know?" I asked.

"Can't you guys just behave?" Ben said.

"I mean that's up to him," I said. "I'm just fine."

"I'm just fine, too," Westley said, spitting more tobacco out everywhere. I thought of hitting him in the mouth, and sometimes I really wish I had. Maybe that would've kept the world from completely spinning out.

But I couldn't have, anyway. Casey opened the car door interrupting.

"Westley, are you done talking yet?" she asked. "The movie's just about to start."

"Finishing up, love," he said, just lively enough to amuse her. She smiled and got back into the car after that. I really don't think I've ever rolled my eyes so hard the way I did in that moment, honestly. "Would you two like to come over sometime?" Westley asked me and Ben, smiling high when he did. "I'd love to have you over."

"Sure, what's your street name again?" Ben asked him.

"It's Harwich Boulevard," Westley told him and then he said, "I'll see you both now," and he got back into his car where Casey was. I never saw Westley again that summer until his house party in September. And then I never saw him again—until today.

He was behind the cash desk at Eisner's, working. I almost didn't realize it was him when I set the David Bowie magazine down alongside my Coke on the counter. He just doesn't look the way he used to. He cuts his hair different and he really seems to have grown into his face a lot.

"Jack Boyd, I can hardly believe it!" he said. His voice rang through every part of the store. I almost jumped from its density.

"Since when did you start working here?" I asked. I forgot he was a year above me, and so he's graduated already.

"Since your good friend Marigold quit without calling," he said. "How is she anyway?"

"Don't talk about Marigold," I said, looking directly at him so he'd know I meant that. "You don't know anything about her."

"Excuse me. I didn't realize it's now bad manners to ask how somebody is."

"Are you capable of having a regular conversation?"

"Are you really asking me that!" he said, also raising his voice when he did. He's always raising his voice and it's so unnecessary.

"When have you ever said anything nice to me?" I asked.

"You'd think I'm the worst goddamn person who's ever lived the way you act toward me, but really, it would turn out you're just goddamn crazy."

He scanned my things, taking a second glance at the David Bowie magazine and looking sick when he did. I didn't know what that was about and I didn't bother asking either. I paid for my things and left quickly.

I rode my bike home the fastest I ever have and my heart beat the fastest it ever has. I thought laying in my bed would help settle that particularity but it didn't work, really. My heart's still at the same high-speed and you'd think I have some empty coffee cup nearby performing this sequence of uneasy things, but I don't have anything.

"I found it scary, that scene in the junkyard mostly," I remember saying to Ben on the drive home from the movie. I really was frightened by that part.

"You find almost everything scary," he said. His car vent whistling some old time, particularly strained melody when he did. "It's kind of fascinating."

"How's that?" I asked.

"I just mean you observe everything pretty well enough to feel some way about it."

It's sad I forgot how to do that anymore.

"I don't know if you're making any sense," I told him.

"I certainly am, you're just not listening right," he said in a sort of comfortable, funny way.

"My bad," I said, taking after his same attitude. "I'll try better."

"That'd be nice, thanks."

Right then, Ben's most favorite song came on the radio, breaking off conversation. "There Is a Light That Never Goes Out" by the Smiths band. He loved that song more than anyone you'd ever know.

"Have you heard this!" he asked—the same way he would every time the song would play anywhere.

"Is it new?" I'd say, only advancing his banter.

He turned it all the way up, clearing out any headroom left for honest conversation, and he sang for a whole hour it seemed, and I decided, really, that I never wanted to go home.

Eventually, though, we arrived at my house, first discovering the end of the song when we did. He turned the radio volume back down to what previous state of listening affairs we'd governed. In the front seat, I dreaded the goodbye. Ben must have felt the same way, thinking about it now. He always did. When he wasn't so absent minded anyway.

"I think Westley's kind of an asshole," I said.

"Oh. He's alright," Ben said. But could I really blame him for not sympathizing—Ben couldn't have noticed anything bad when it was so distinguished looking. Even if it were bleeding all over the place and ruining the teal covering. He'd known Westley longer than I had anyway.

I looked out the car window at my house. I remember hearing footsteps on the porch stairs uttering in perfect agreement—quiet because they'd come to know me better than anybody had—your heart's too meaningful. Stop that and write sentences of poetry about stopping that. It's hard to explain, really, but everything after came so easy and how I'd known it before.

I felt the car vent warm again.

"Thanks for inviting me out," I said. "And for buying my ticket."

"I'm always glad to," he said. "And I mean that."

I couldn't ever be mad at him for anything. He was too goddamn nice. Sadly, though, I was stunned by the cracking in my bedroom window from the world so demanding and slow, that I'd learned how to aim just right. I could burn everything around me had I really wanted to. Nothing seemed important to keep once I'd known my mom was dying anyway.

"Maisie's probably called," I said. "I had better go look."

"Right," Ben said, concentrating on his steering wheel if it were something extraordinary to hide his feelings well. "I'll call you tomorrow sometime."

"I'll look forward to it the whole day then," I said. He looked over at me, fighting off a smile. It just about killed me.

"I won't keep you waiting."

"You're too kind," I said, very polite about it when I did, but I was really telling him that, hoping he'd listen. I opened the car door and got out. I remember the sky outside a clear sight.

"Wait! How was my driving?" he asked, right before I could close the door and reflect on the evening just myself.

"You're learning certainly, of course, and you'll get there, probably," I said, making him laugh when I did. I should've told him to never drive again. I could have saved him from the shortened life span. Across everything I've confessed to you, allying what brute memory I've forfeited too, I might regret this moment the most.

I told him goodbye, retiring confidence in my own embarrassing manners for the moment I did. I could be mean, yes, but never during the goodbye process. He smiled, the night's parting gift, and settled the goodbye. I closed the door of the car at the sound of that.

I got up to my house, the house lights so blinding and the first porch step creaking deceptive notes of the night, putting me at great distance from him. I went inside my house, hearing his car drive off when I did, and I should have looked back at him, but I didn't. Is it enough to wish I really had?

A light was on in the living room. I found my mom awake still, sitting on the recliner, impossibly curious in a book taking position on her lap and the coffee pot seemingly just made on the table. I was surprised seeing this, balancing some dismay too, because she shouldn't be staying up so late when she's feeling sick.

She looked up almost immediately when I came into the room.

"Jack! How was your night?" she asked. She enjoyed asking you things like that so very much all the time. She just really liked knowing about you. Striking conversation was her best factor and that's not something easy everybody can do.

"You didn't have to stay up," I told her.

"I don't mind it," she said, folding over the corner of the latest page in her book and closing it. She put it aside on the table, reserving attention for just our conversation. "I wanted to hear about your night. How was the movie?"

"It was good, though a little scary," I said.

"Was it?" she asked. "I wouldn't have thought so. Did Ben not want to come inside?"

"I didn't ask him to."

I sat down on the living room floor and began taking my shoes off. I'd double knotted them.

"You haven't had him over in a little while," she said.

"Ben's fine."

"You're allowed to have him over, Jack."

"I know."

"I don't want you thinking because I'm sick that he's not allowed over anymore."

"It's not that," I said. I couldn't seem to figure out the double knot, I remember. My mom saw my frustration, and fair sighted, right through it too, the way she saw almost everything.

"Jack, stop. Before you hurt your fingers." So I gave up. "What are you upset about?"

I paused, reasoning the world and just about everything when I did. Where do you start when asked that?

At the very beginning—helpless, new and so young.

My mom got up from the recliner and hugged me. I began crying and pretty hard, too. I had everything to cry to neatly lined up against the wall. I let them have at the canvas in any color they wanted. I was feeling too exhausted anyway.

"Slow down and breathe, Jack." She put her hand on my chest. Pressing lightly, she paced my breathing. My heartbeat wrestled some return to its regular schedule. "Right now you just have to breathe. Nothing else."

And so that's what I did.

Eventually the world slowed down and I was just fine. My mom fixed my shoelaces after and put my shoes away into the closet. I cleaned my face in the kitchen sink while she did that.

"Do you want coffee?" she asked, coming back into the room. "Or you should have some water, I suppose." She went over to the cabinet and got out a glass. I noticed her hands kind of shaking holding it. She used the faucet to fill it up, but must not have paid very good attention because some flowed right out of the cup. I didn't say anything though of course. I just held a wet glass.

But anyway, the house was all back to quiet work again, and that's when I first got to hear a real life songbird. I'll keep that memory safe forever if I can.

"What is that?" I asked.

"I think it could be a songbird," my mom said, whispering. She had this big expression on her face.

She was just so excited about it. She opened the window above the sink all the way it could open that she broke it, actually. My dad still needs to fix it today. "Be so quiet!" she said as we both tried not to laugh.

I held my breath, setting my water glass down on the counter. And the noise seemed to get closer. I listened the most careful I ever have at the songbird and his task so peaceful and sound as the clouds in nighttime are.

"Isn't that wonderful?" my mom asked. "I just wish I could hear it all the time."

"That would be nice," I said.

Every night that summer, we listened out through the window for the songbirds. We heard them a couple times more, but not so often. On their nights absent, my mom sang "Songbird" by Fleetwood Mac instead, as though that'd get them to come back.

"They must not hear you," I told her. "Raise your voice just somewhat."

"I'd better not," she said. Catching her breath had increased difficulty by then. And by then I looked at every night as the last time we'd get to hear the songbirds together.

I'd gotten a blank cassette tape from Eisner's to record the songbirds when she went to the hospital so she could listen some other way—but they just never sang again. So instead, and you might find this stupid anyway, I had Ben whistle into the microphone his favorite song. My mom absolutely loved it so much that she cried. I played the recording at her funeral and it became the saddest thing. I don't know where I've put that tape at today. I wish I did.

Sorry—I don't mean to be so tragic. I'll quit that now.

It's gotten late in the afternoon, meaning that everyone at school should be finding themselves back home, and so Marigold should be over in a little while. She said she'd stop by. I'll open my curtains just in case she does anyway. I've had them shut for some time. It's gotten awfully dark in here.

Chapter 8:

It's a New Life, Right?

February had surprised everyone.

It was warm enough outside, I remember, to leave the window open in the drawing room this one particular day—I want you to remember that, so write it down if you have to. I'm making it easy enough.

"You were gone a while. Who's your new friend?" Ansel asked the very moment I came back to our room. He saw me on the stairs with Maisie, apparently. "Is she that girl you love?"

"What makes you think that?" I asked him.

"I've come to know you well enough," he said. "And she's just how you described." He said that last part in the worst British accent you'd ever hear. "I heard you both talking out on the stairs."

"Do you listen in on everything?"

"Mostly, yes. Has that become a problem now?"

"When it has nothing to do with you, yes. How have you not taken that off yet?" I'd noticed he was wearing the jacket I'd given him for when we'd gone outside—still.

"It's cold. You're just warm from being in Miss Penny's office and it's a goddamn steam bath in there so you don't notice it. How's your hands?"

"Oh, they're fine," I said, looking at them and the sticking plaster Maisie applied. "Just a little bruised."

"But how ever are you supposed to self-abuse!" he said. "I couldn't live a day without doing it. Suppose it's good you've got your girlfriend now."

"You're a dirty moron," I told him. "And she's not my girlfriend. I never said that."

"My bad assuming the girl you told me kissing stories about isn't your girlfriend."

"Those stories weren't anything important," I said, having just kissed Maisie again minutes before. I don't know why I couldn't be honest. Everything would be so different, maybe, if I had. I don't think I'd be writing you, though. Certainly not. And there'd be no exciting color blue.

"Oh, well, they were fascinating. I wish you had more," Ansel said.

"So you could self-abuse?" I asked, only teasing him.

"But I'm a dirty moron!"

"You are, thanks for admitting that."

I'm trying to remember every detail I can—Ansel was laying on his bed, studying the ceiling—his face was red from the freezing weather. But what was I doing? I had something in my eye—yes, that's right. I had a little dust particle out from the quiet corner blurring the whole landscape of things. I blinked and I blinked again but it didn't go anywhere. So I went into the bathroom, and in the mirror, I pulled my eyelid down, retrieving the little dust splinter. Feeling nothing, I flicked it away once I did. My eyesight back and proper again, I decided I'd stare at myself in the mirror for a while. Above my lip, my scar was looking extra fine and bright, for some reason, and it brought memory of terrible September happenings. I looked all over the place for that dust particle back, in every drawer and dressing table crevice, but something hit the ceiling light, putting me outside in the dark again. I was walking up to Westley Reid's house. Ben was talking.

"How's your lip feeling?" he asked.

"About the same it did when you asked me two streets ago," I told him. I'd taken the band aid off for the party and he was very concerned about that, I remember. I wish I didn't find that so unnecessary then. I'd accept his concern and put it in some glass jar with a tulip out for show if I still had it today.

"Just making sure. Should we stay long?" he asked. He meant should we stay long at Westley's party.

"I don't know, if you'd like to," I said.

I have cause to regret everything.

Westley Reid lives on Harwich Boulevard, and so I find it to be the worst goddamn street in Cradock. I have that reason and the sidewalks being perfectly flat, too. It's unnerving—and so is the very thought of the wooden stop sign post at the end of Harwich Boulevard broken in half still. I don't think anyone's ever coming to fix it, and I can't blame them, really. Most things end up broken anyway. Don't you know that yet?

Westley's house is big and he has a swimming pool and his parents had gone that weekend to see the Monkees in Birmingham, and so he reserved the house specially for a party. Everyone young was there of course and everyone was young in their activities too. It was the first time I ever drank a "White Lightning." Do you know what that is? It's a very cheap alcohol, I was told anyway, and it's pretty alright. I'd probably never drink it again now, though. It would only leave a bad taste, remembering.

As we came up to his house, outside on the lawn, there were kids already going stupid, running around and jumping on each other, despite the sun not having fully set. I was never that young to do any of that, and writing about it now, I wish I were. Could I try again someday?

"Where's Maisie tonight?" Ben asked.

"Babysitting. She said she might come by," I said. "Is Marigold on her way?"

"Should be. Oh, don't mention that I kissed you earlier, by the way. Even if it was just to save your goddamn life. I don't know how Marigold would feel about that."

"About saving my goddamn life or that we kissed?" I joked.

"I won't answer you that," he said, joking too. At least I thought he was in that moment anyway.

Suddenly I found my name being shouted at a very high volume across the lawn. I looked over, to absolutely no surprise, at Westley Reid standing in his doorway. Wearing no shirt, he had only some kind of feathery blonde scarf on.

"JACK BOYD!" he was yelling. "JACK BOYD IS AT MY HOUSE! CAN YOU EVER BELIEVE THAT!"

He came down his porch steps, explicitly smug and his eyes so vacant ahead of the night at hand. I put my best smile on—this had become a reflex around Westley because I'd somewhat accepted his friendship with Ben—and I told myself I wasn't going to be troublesome that night anyway. I'm really so glad I wasn't.

"Hi, Westley," I said. "Having a fun night already?"

"DAMN RIGHT I AM!" he was yelling for no good reason still because he was there right in front of me now. I wiped his goddamn spit off my face, feeling violated when I did. He turned away to Ben and put his hands on Ben's shoulders, shaking him. "LOVELY BEN!"

"I can hear you, Westley!" Ben said.

"Lovely, lovely Ben. You're looking very attractive tonight. Don't you think, Jack?" He looked back over at me, just to give the most unpleasant wink. I've never known anyone who struggles winking the way he does. "Is Marigold expected tonight?"

"I think so," Ben said, looking at me in a manner suggesting he wanted some relief from the grip Westley had on his shoulders.

"Ben and I are going to find something to drink," I said. I knew that would excite Westley enough to let Ben go.

"I'm never opposed to that," Westley said, letting go of Ben finally. "You two find your calling!"

We set off inside, leaving Westley and his goddamn scarf out on the lawn behind. And if only it were that way forever.

Music was playing so loud coming from every corner in the house it seemed. I think, if you were there perhaps, you'd begin writing the neighbor's an apology to give them the next day. I would have anyway if other things to worry about hadn't delivered themselves in the worst cardboard giftbox ever.

"I can't hear anything. Can you hear anything?" Ben said.

"Must be why Westley came out yelling then," I said.

"No, he's just that annoying."

"I've never heard you call anyone that," I said. He laughed, though I could barely hear it through the music, but I saw him smile at least.

"I'm making a new life," Ben said, and it's almost funny, him saying that so unknowing.

We found our way to the kitchen eventually, through everybody dancing. In there we saw Casey Morris.

"Hi, Casey," I said, just being polite. I never liked her that much anyway. I think I told you that already, though.

"Hey, you two. Did you just get here?" she asked. She was drinking from a straw she'd put in a bottle. I didn't know the use in that.

"Apparently so," I said. "I didn't expect so many people to be here already. It's not dark out yet."

"What's there a rule to when a party can start?" she asked, taking a sip out of her straw. I found this little thing quite very annoying and so unnecessarily prim. I think that's a great word to describe Casey Morris, actually—prim. If only you knew her at all.

"What do you have to drink?" Ben asked, interrupting all of a sudden. I think he knew I'd probably say something mean if he didn't.

"Aw, Ben. Everything. What do you crave?" she asked him.

"Could I just have a Coke?" he said.

"No, that's boring!" she told him. "Can I put some vodka in it if you're doing that?"

"I'm good, thanks. Just a straight Coke, please."

"You're not any fun, Ben Coleridge. What about you, Jack? What are you having tonight?"

"I don't know, anything. You pick," I said.

"Oh gladly!" She went over to the refrigerator, opened it, and that's where the "White Lightning" I told you about came from. Casey handed it to me, saying, "I think you'll absolutely love this, and we have so many if you do because they're not expensive at all. And the Cokes are out in the garage, so I'll be right back."

Ben and I waited. I opened the White Lightning while we did and drank some of it—too much at my first sip. I didn't know anything about how to drink alcohol properly because I'd never drank anything before. I remember I had this strong burning feeling in my throat right after. But you get used to it. I know I did anyway.

"Do you like it?" Ben asked.

"It's alright," I said. "I think I'd rather have a Coke, honestly."

He laughed—how I wish I could write the sound notes to that and learn the piano and fumble playing them around the house whenever. It would be perfect living and the sun would come up again every day.

Casey came back, one glassy bottled Coke in hand. It was opened already.

"For you, Ben," she said, giving it to him. She had the biggest smile on her face and I should've known she was playing some terrible game. But I didn't know anything.

"Thanks a lot, Casey," he said.

"You're so welcome. When's Marigold coming?" she asked—that same stupid horrible smile yet to leave us and the room alone. I really should've known. It was so very obvious anyway. Have you noticed it yet?

"Well, she should be on her way now. I remember her saying she'd come before eight," he told her. "What time is it now?"

"It's seven thirty!" Casey outright exclaimed. "Oh, Ben, we have to dance before she gets here! Are you interested in dancing?"

"I really don't think I'd better," he said.

"Don't be boring! You're already so boring. Everyone's dancing. Even Jack's dancing."

"No, I'm not," I said.

"But you're going to! Aren't you?"

"Could I finish my drink first?" I asked.

"Bring it with you! And Ben you bring your Coke! You're both coming dancing. It's settled."

"It's only half settled," I said. "Ben doesn't want to."

I looked at Ben, smiling politely, for example, how a little kid wanting a high risk, yet most simple favor would. I was seven again, repeating to myself favorite rhymes in the window's reflecting surface. Stopping at words that didn't fit, burning a candle, breaking my brain, improving vocabulary. Every night was the same kind of beautiful fastening. Some things float better unchanged.

"Oh, damn you," he said, joking of course. "Fine!"

"You're cute boys," Casey said. "But the trouble is I have a boyfriend. Do you know where he's at? He was wearing my scarf."

"I saw him outside," I told her.

"What's he doing out there?" she asked, suddenly leaving me and Ben in the kitchen by just ourselves. Her mind, I decided, was everywhere but her mind. And she couldn't walk in a very straight line.

"So are we not dancing?" Ben said.

"Absolutely we're dancing. Don't you want to?"

"I'm not very good."

"Oh, well, I'm the goddamn best," I said, taking his hand that wasn't holding the Coke bottle, and leading him to the living room made up of so many young adults whose brains were changing. In there the music was especially loud and suffocating. I let it hug the very thought of everything—what a practice so comforting—and then came the very most perfect thing.

Ben's favorite song was playing.

He paused, looked at me if for some kind of goddamn approval, only amusing himself a little, and then danced self-possessed. Carefully enough, though, so as to not spill out his drink or hurt anybody. You wouldn't know him to ever hurt anybody. So forget the newspaper headings, they don't know anything.

I danced beside him, pressing closely against him, just like I had some few hours before at the creek, and the physical energy was beautiful probably from those onlooking. I felt, for possibly one of the last times, the relationship of bright, daring sparks flying and flying apart. My conscience delivered lovely appearing on my face. You would have thought I was a madman from my smiling. But what else was I to do anyway? My strongest and darkest muscle had died for a moment and I was going to celebrate that of course. Wouldn't you have?

When the song ended and there was that fleeting moment before the next song came on, Ben could ask me softly, all out of breath though, "Do you think we should go somewhere more quiet?" I agreed right away of course. He could ask me anything—jump off a bridge into the ocean meant only for washing out the water supply—and I'd do it.

We found ourselves upstairs, stumbling over the carpet, running and losing some of my drink on the railing. I'm realizing now that I never saw Ben drink from his Coke—but he must have at some point that night or the tiny bronze string I've put into every margin of this story is only a tiny bronze string—useless and tightening. It's so important you remember that.

"Is that Westley?" Ben asked, pointing to a dust-covered, framed glass, dwelling photograph on the wall of a little kid holding a candy cigarette. I hoped it was candy anyway.

"How'd they know him so far in advance?" I asked, making Ben laugh so crazily when I did.

"I want to find his room," Ben said, aspiring to pronounce his own particular words. "Can we find his room?"

"We had better not get caught," I told him.

"I'm not ever worrying about that," he said. He started up laughing again.

"Brave man," I said, following him down the hallway after.

Westley's bedroom was somewhere on the right of the amazing house. I don't remember, honestly, and that detail's not so worth your attention, so forget I mentioned that anyway. I've drawn focus, and single curtains too, the wrong places many times before. Did you even notice, turning the handle on the bedroom door, Ben no longer had his Coke refreshment?

Even upstairs you could hear the music well enough still. Ben closed the door, silencing it a little, and I could hear my heartbeat normally again—playing with every good second, tapping fingers on the hollow red wooden desk. I must have left it there or something. Just around the corner, or something. I wonder where it's at tonight.

"Isn't this better?" Ben asked.

"Much quieter, yeah, thanks," I said. "How do you think Westley would react knowing we're in here?"

"It doesn't matter! Westley and his fucking scarf," Ben said, collapsing onto Westley's striped bed fitted sheets—probably the dirtiest thing you could ever lay on, but I collapsed next to him anyway. "I can't believe Westley and his fucking scarf. Can you?"

My cheeks were feeling red, I remember, and the ceiling was moving around in ring shapes, getting married.

"I don't believe anything right now," I said. I was seeing many different groups of heaven and not a single one felt safe. I was so dizzy, walking the gravel path so fast and slow-moving. I wanted to close my eyes long.

"Oh, that's reasonable. I want to get under the covers. I'm just freezing."

I looked at him, confused, hearing footsteps out of sync on the roof outside. Were they toe dancing?

"Have you gone mad?" I asked him. "You want to get under Westley Reid's bed covers? Do you know what bugs live under there?"

"Relax, Jack! Relax. What's the matter? You and I have slept together before."

"You've absolutely gone mad."

"Doesn't everybody after some time?" he said, sitting up. Leaning against the bedframe, he began taking off his shirt involving buttons.

"Now what are you doing?" I asked.

"I don't like sleeping with a shirt on. I thought you knew that. Why are you looking sick?"

"Because you're out of your mind completely!"

"Stop accusing me of that. I told you it's a new life."

He couldn't figure out the top button, I remember. His fingers were one after the other by the collar, changing direction all over, competing against just themselves for the prize. I couldn't handle seeing this troubled moment in the nearby high quality, and so I sat up on the bed and leaned towards him.

"Well, if it's a new life, we have to celebrate that somehow," I said, unbuttoning the top button easy for him. Looking at him was funny, I remember, because my eyesight was never blurry when I did. It was sharp and I had a clearer understanding more than ever.

"Sleeping first," he said, taking his shirt all the way off and tossing it onto the floor. Lifting up the bed covers, he got under them. He patted the open space beside him. He was smiling blind, his past life's best work born again. "Are you coming with?"

"You're so convincing. It's magnificent, honestly." And so I lowered myself under the bed covers, too, probably sacrificing my youth when I did, too. But it really didn't matter, childhood was over anyway, and I've since adjusted my periphery view on the work of dirty bedsheets today.

Ben was humming "Just Born in Manhattan."

"Do you know the song?" he asked.

"Sure thing. Do you know me at all?" I said.

"I know you better than anybody does. You're the best friend I've ever had. Did you know that?"

"You might have told me before, but I almost forgot anyway, so thanks for telling me."

"Am I the best friend you've ever had?" he asked.

"I think you're the only friend I've ever had," I told him.

"Oh, I doubt that very much," he said. "What about Maisie and Marigold? Aren't they your friends?"

"I know they're my friends of course, but I don't know. I don't know what I'm saying."

"That's alright. I'll keep it a secret." He winked, so charming and so terrible as hell, at me. It had gotten darker outside now and the overhead light was never on, so he couldn't have noticed my cheeks glowing so rosy and embarrassed, but I was afraid that he might anyway. I was never in the habit of being afraid around him and so you'd have to forgive me, but what was happening suddenly? I'm traveling in blue, striped, white silk stockings and staying at the best hotels all of a sudden, hardly knowing the people I'm sleeping in beds with. But I met them at a party once before, and I'm half in love with them, and it was too cold to sleep apart and across the room. I told myself I was sad and amusing myself, and finally that my best friend laying undressed beside myself was crazy himself.

"Oh, well, thanks," I said. "Do you have a best secret?"

"Hm. What are you asking that for?"

"For me to also keep a secret," I told him.

"I'd have to think about it. Can I think about it?"

"I have no proper bedtime, so yes."

And so he went on thinking about it, in his skull running red, blue and wild probably. I listened to him breathing while he did. Breathing in and out at a pretty regular pace, better than I'd known him for usually doing. He was so calm, the middle of the afternoon, giving all the rage a little kick so good and interesting that it fell onto the gravel and dematerialized.

"I don't know if I have a best secret, exactly," he said after a bit of mind reasoning in a very quiet voice. I almost couldn't hear him.

"Are you whispering?" I asked.

"Oh, yes, well, we're telling secrets," he said, whispering. "It's only appropriate we go all in." I laughed.

"I'll whisper too, then."

"That's good, good," he said, decreasing his volume again on the second "good." I was listening to the coming poem miles away—a year away, actually, it seemed, on the edge of multiple cliffsides. I moved over closer to him, so as to hear him well enough then. I found my shoulder hitting his every time one of us would breathe, as if we were dancing again. It was delightful in my experience of dreams, and I never found his voice so conspiring of textured water steaming and soft light napping on the doorway. "My best secret, if I'm going to be honest, is that I didn't mind kissing you earlier. It was sort of nice."

I paused in my breathing activity. Wouldn't you have? When all the light you've ever known is in some blur of discovery on the left side of the bed, several yards out to sea rocking past world ending demise. You'd want to sing something else, or find a new line of words and work. So many times, over and over the tall height again, you've ignored the door creaking. You've thought it must be some kind of brave imagination. You've balanced any pressing mean that would outweigh the truth, neglecting your irregular heartbeat pattern so much that there's blood everywhere on every page and every theme now. Are you hoping to squeeze your heart clear of wrong trouble? Cut off the blood going—stop the progress? It's not so easy, and life's never so boring.

I sat up straight, and I kissed him straight, letting my heart beat on the side of everything perfect. Feeling the bright, daring sparks flying and flying apart. Leaving any poorly made judgement behind.

I wasn't discovering anything new. I knew him, and the necessary angles of his body, flexible as spring. I put my hand on his tough stomach muscle, and felt him breathing in the freedom of dying physical expression. He put his hand up the backside of my shirt and pulled me in closer towards him, all-knowing of all things kissing. His fingers moved to play with the edges of my hair, messing it up completely, and repeating the same process after. I believed in everything and him only, whatever deep thing that means.

I broke the kiss off only so I could breathe. I suppose I don't know anything about how to kiss the right ways. I'm collecting sharp end dollar tips this whole time.

"What's up?" Ben asked, totally cool and fully grown like we hadn't just tossed our eleven year agreement into the company of high priced wastebaskets Westley kept by his nightstand. I glanced at them a couple of times that night, never understanding why he'd need that many. He must be filthy.

"I just needed to breathe," I told him.

"Were you not breathing?"

"I couldn't. How are you?"

"Oh, well you know, it's easy. I think of it like I'm swimming."

"What could you possibly mean?"

He put his hand up to my chest, and I thought of him as my teacher, better looking than any one that I've had of course.

"Hold your breath," he said. And so I did. "Now let go but through your nose."

"That doesn't feel right," I said.

"Just breathe through your nose." He picked up kissing me again for a moment, soft and combing my hair, then he pulled away. "Breathing?" he asked.

"Out through my nose," I said, lying. I was practically smoking myself to death. I just couldn't understand what he meant about swimming. It didn't make any sort of good sense, but then nothing that night did anyway.

We got back to kissing ordinary after, but I felt the excitement dwindling almost, undergoing series of lukewarm change. Stars falling away. Books closing on the worst page. Water flooding midtown, taking window shop glass out and leaving it be on the crescent shaped street. I was splashing around in the water remaining—cutting my feet and the cord of my darling life. Could this do forever? I thought while kissing him. I'd felt the madness so exhilarating letting fireworks off, but the ash in due course was making it hard to breathe.

So I broke the kiss off again, on the better reasoning that he was my best friend and space was plenty infinite, and the world loving him required so much more than I could ever give. My heart was too dull and broken. Even put back together after a whole decade, it would never beat again the same and never be strong enough for loving him. Writing that is the most honest I've ever lived. It's only taken my whole life.

"What time do you think it is?" I asked him. "Feels like we left the party hours ago."

Ben looked at me, thinking noticeably on his beautiful face. I could have stared all mornings, reading by sense, stiff as a carboard giftbox, lowering the blinds at the starting point of the best spring. But I was too afraid of everything and I was never told, really, the beginning date of spring. I always forget anyway. And it seems to be different every year.

He reached over to the nightstand, taking hold of Westley's electric clock and showing me it.

"Not even twenty minutes we've been gone," he said. He set the clock back on its nightstand location.

"Oh, just felt a lot longer."

"You're bad at telling time."

"Well that's alright. It's not my job or anything."

Abbreviated silence stylized itself in the room, writing off notice as we both forgot what we were saying before at once. I was never good at inventing meaningful conversation after these fumbling moments. I couldn't follow a regular talking process if I were taught how. I always seem to make it worse than ever intended.

"It's quite late, though," I said. It was only about eight, according to the number available upon the clock anyway. "Do you think Marigold's here yet?"

"I don't know. Maybe," he said. "Is that what you're thinking about?"

"I don't know. Maybe." He sighed. "Have I ruined your night?"

"You could never ruin my night," he swore—but I very well could, I'm thinking. I could ask you about going home early, and in your car we're wandering, and you discover I can ruin absolutely everything if I concentrate enough. As one day I feared you would.

"I'm not sorry for kissing you back," he said then. "Just to let you know."

"I hope you wouldn't be," I said. What poor advancement of encouragement, representing the worst of all historical time.

"Well, anyway. I should find my shirt."

He got out of the bed and found his shirt on the floor. I sat there unmoving, remembering difficulty of the whole past month. My mind used to always love going there—beyond the worst place and down the river stream of terrible imagining so insistent of terrible imagining. I could never do anything about it.

"You don't seem alright," Ben said then. He was putting his shirt back on and not taking his eyes off of me while he did so. His work by hand was interesting in view that he didn't know anything about working the top button before, but now he could neglect mindful eyes from every button and dedicate that instead to the seeming belief that I was back in danger down the river stream. "I have to know how you're feeling."

"Why's that?" I asked him.

"Because, Jack, you're my best friend. I have to know everything about you."

"Is that part of the craft?"

"I've always thought so, yeah." He finished buttoning everything but the top button—of course leaving that custom for me especially. "Do you mind?" he asked, signing hands towards the button. He sat on the bed and turned sideways facing me, eyes taking after the darkest night and comforting spite.

"You can't do anything yourself," I said, moving to the end of the bed, reaching for his collar and fastening the button when I got there.

"Well, I have you for that reason." He smiled outside a darling line, asking himself—it seemed, up to what point could he go that maybe I'd kiss him again. And I know that, yes, I should have kissed him again, but my employing affective participation was at the worst circumstance. "So now you'll tell me what has you so blue," he said.

"It wasn't kissing you," I told him.

"Oh, well, that's very good to know." He hit his knee against mine, light and creased as a mining bee living on old age, specifying they do not like to sting. "I thought we're telling secrets. Did I get confused?"

"You must have," I said, teasing him rightfully back. And then I got quiet, the cycle starting again, letting just the music from downstairs hang onto the moment alone—for a short time only, though. "Nothing's the same. Do you feel it that way?" I asked him.

He was thinking, humming an original blue shade vaguely.

"Nothing was ever going to be the same," he said soon afterward. "And that's not your fault or mine."

"I know."

"No, you don't—stop that, actually. You don't have to constantly know everything."

"I can't help doing that."

"Nothing's the same! Nothing's the same and we can't do anything about that!" he said in a very piercing whisper that just about threw me off the bed scared. "What did you have in mind anyway?"

"I don't know. I just thought we'd never change. I look at myself in the mirror sometimes and don't know that person or anything. And my eyes just look glossed over all the time like I spend the middle of every night crying."

"I like your eyes," he said.

"You're lying. You're kind, though."

"Sometimes, Jack, I wonder if you know me at all."

"Oh. Why's that?" I asked.

"You dismiss lots that I say, even though I'm saying exactly what you want. What if I said I loved you? You'd say that I've gone mad and I'm completely out of my mind for my own understanding. But I love you Jack, and I need you to listen for just a minute. We don't keep secrets. I've never kept a secret from you, and yet, when I ask how's your day, you keep everything out of it. You could break every bone in your finger and not once mention it. Knowing you is important to me but you're not letting me anymore. I know you've had a bad summer and I'd give my life to fix that and have you sleep through the night. Why are you so against that?"

It's too complex management, I thought, and I never asked him to carry the heaviness of my grief and certainly not to kill himself over it. I should have let him know that, but everything got all swept away in the wind's cold melody before I could. And the pieces were hard to pick apart from the broken glass covering the pavement surface already, and it was so dark that I could hardly see to begin anyway. Harwich Boulevard has only two working streetlamps.

"I don't need your pitying. And I'm not tired," I told him.

"I wasn't asking permission, and I don't believe that for a moment." He glanced dangerously at me, no longer careful of the high wire cord put above everything. I felt confined by the world and my muscles never had good experience—was jumping the only proper course of measurement left? He's my best friend, and he's kind and his heart's very soft and so easygoing on the worst days you've ever had.

I take my best standing start.

"What do you want to know?" I asked.

Downstairs, the party was still going, well-built energy across the living room space. We saw Marigold over by the television set.

"Fancy seeing you both here," she said once we'd gotten out of the whole dancing network and finally over to her. Ben was carrying his drink in hand again, I'd noticed. I don't quite have any idea when he might have picked that back up, or if he'd ever set it down to start off. I wasn't focused on that specific thing anyway, but rather the young kiss Marigold was placing on Ben's cheek instead, and the heightening possibility of my brain in every bright colored flame. I had found Ben looking at me when she did that, and so I looked quickly away at the blank television screen, watching the reflection of everyone dancing. Stepping apart from the other across the flat carpet and gathering again, better aware of separation. "What are you drinking?" she asked, picking up his hand. "Oh, you're drinking a Coke, of course, I should have known. What about you, Jack? Have you gotten a drink?"

"I have, yes," I said. "Though I must have left it upstairs."

"What were you doing upstairs?" she asked. My eyes were not brave enough to leave the television screen or gaze absent at anything the whole time. I felt my cheeks burning, outpouring red glittering.

"I was looking for the bathroom," I told her, saving the dreadful conversation arriving for a later date eventually.

"Did you find it?"

"Oh, yes. I did."

"Are you feeling okay? Your cheeks are looking pink."

"I'm alright. Just a little warm."

"Oh, well, Westley has a pool out back! Do you guys want to swim?" she asked. "It would cool you right off probably."

"I don't have my swimsuit currently," I said.

"Wear your boxer shorts! Hasn't ever stopped you before."

"I don't know how I feel about doing that in front of a big crowd."

"Oh, you're good looking enough, Jack!" she said. "The only worst thing that could happen is your analyzing too much!"

"I don't know," I said, looking at Ben and asking him, "What are you thinking?" He smiled many things.

"I could swim," he said, rolling down the sleeves of his shirt from his elbows. I wasn't necessarily up for it, but my muscles gave way and I smiled right back. Haven't I told you I'd once do anything Ben did?

Westley's pool lights were on, flashing different colors every couple of seconds, illuminating the awning of different green lines connecting. A lot of people were in the pool swimming and there was more music coming from someplace nearby. I just couldn't find where.

From the side, Ben got quiet in my hearing length, asking me, "Are you swimming?" and telling me, "You don't have to if you're not wanting to. I heard it's going to rain anyway."

"Really, I'm fine," I told him. "It's a new life, right?"

Marigold was taking off her clothes, debuting the same bright fleecy red color undergarments. Ben unbuttoned his shirt again, and in my boxer shorts, I folded my clothes, leaving them neatly off to the side on a pool chair Westley had.

With almost nothing on, Marigold jumped in the pool first and Ben followed right after of course. I contemplated my every decision up to that point, and then obeyed the requirements of a new life. I felt I had everything special to do.

Late at night, below the water especially, I am qualified for anyone—anything. I was holding my breath, thinking of what Ben said, and the terrible accuracy of that statement. Kissing's not like swimming. I didn't know where he ever got that from, until a spring day in February, running too late behind time at that time.

I came up from the water, young in all of my best glory, and swam over to where Ben and Marigold were hanging out.

"Have you cooled off any?" Marigold asked. Her red garments reflected the top of the water very well, honestly, I remember, and made her breasts look very large, and greater than normal. I found that very attractive, and later scolded my own brain for the horrible advocate it had become.

"The water's fine," I said.

"What do you mean by fine? It's so wonderful!" she said, putting her head back in the water, facing up toward the night sky. I decided to do the same, and when I did, I swore the stars were winking at me. Was it that, or the effect of bright daring sparks flying apart?

"Are the stars winking at you guys?" I asked. I heard them both laugh. "I swear they're winking at me! That one there!" I pointed to some indefinite place in the sky because there were many stars everywhere that night, and you could pick any one of them and find them winking at me. I swear that you could.

"You're not thinking straight," Ben said. "But when have you ever?"

"You always do too much talking!" I said right away after.

He returned with, "You live in a glass house!"

"Both of you stop talking," Marigold cut in, making a hushing noise shortly just after. "Shh and look at the stars. I find them so wonderful."

So we looked at the wonderful city of big name stars, lonely living up there above everything—but at least they have each other to keep company. I had my best friends doing the same. I only noticed that when it was far too late and sharp, no longer meaning anything and slicing open my finger when I felt it.

It wasn't peaceful very long. Westley's voice filled the outer background and in a moment he was jumping into the pool, sending waves our way, forcing us to leave the stars up there behind.

He began shouting in the same manner from earlier as though we hadn't noticed him or anything. "MY BEAUTIFUL GUESTS I'VE COME OUTSIDE!"

"Find a different place!" Ben shouted at him. Westley splashed water at him, and Ben did the same thing. They did that for a little while, splashing water at each other, playing like boys, neon chlorinating their eyes.

It was a summer night and a new life, right and brilliant enough to the very bitter end. I'm reading my words over to find the stopping place, tracing my finger over the page, where I could have saved my best friend. Maybe it was the pool water in his eyes, drying them out and blinding him.

"Can you guys stop it?" Marigold said. "How old are you both?"

"Age isn't a very important matter," Westley said back to her. Him saying that was funny, keeping in mind the rumors that you'd find going around about Westley each week claiming a new freshmen girl he was sleeping in bed with. I always wondered Casey's opinion on this, but never cared so much to ask.

Ben did stop splashing the water, though of course. He followed instructions well, especially those given by Marigold. He swam over to Marigold and kissed her shoulder, exactly right by the string line of her red garment. I couldn't decide my very desire, whether it was her or him or a passage fused with sweet wording.

"You two love birds had better find a room," Westley said to them, and then of course his concern found property near at hand. "Where's your lover girl?" he asked me, annoying in the process of asking.

"I could ask you the very same," I said. "Did she take your scarf from you?" I noticed he wasn't wearing that scarf anymore.

"I gave it back."

"I'm certain that's what happened."

"Well, yes, matter of fact, that is what happened, Jack. Do you have trouble understanding that?"

"No, but your explaining is poor. I'd work a little on that before anything else." He laughed.

"I forget you're a funny guy!" he said.

"Oh, that's kind of worrying."

"What is?"

"How often you seem to forget," I said. He laughed again.

"You're good, Jack Boyd. You're a damn good funny man."

"What are you both talking about?" Ben interrupted, saving me nicely.

"Just how funny I am, apparently," I said.

"I've always said you're very funny!" Marigold joined in, giving more praise all of a sudden. I was feeling equally unique and blue.

"Oh, thanks, Marigold," I said. I don't remember whether my cheeks got red as her garments, but they might have. You couldn't have known in the pool light's developing pattern anyway. They were bright, yes, but dim enough to get away with humbled glowing. I saw Ben looking at me, though, sharp as the edge curving of a picture frame. I never got away with anything involving him. Forget humbled glowing. I had sharp eyes going directly at me, through me, inside of me, inspecting the residence of my heart rate beating. From what I remember, it was at full tilt with all the speed of rough treatment, beating all the wrong ways. And I couldn't do a thing about it, or the rain that started by chance—thankfully.

We wiped dry inside. Westley had unlimited toweling it seemed. I put my clothes back on, making sure that I didn't look at Marigold dressing because I could feel Ben's eyes glaring tiny knives still, supposing reference marks every time. My attempt to dry off had completely achieved nothing leaving my boxers very much damp, causing uncomfortable shifting in my jeans later.

"Everyone gather around," Westley said, turning the music all the way down, making the room so quiet except for lungs breathing. "I have a game in mind."

I sat on the living room floor next to Ben and Marigold of course. Ben sat in the middle, the dividing line between us—it's very important to note that so to make easier the activities of the game, and the matter of kissing mouth techniques that I'm about to explain.

With almost everyone settled throughout the living room and around the high-end, clear glass coffee table, Westley placed a bottle onto the table's plate surface, set empty for spinning.

Pleased cheering and the sad wiring of a birdcage hissing occurred from a handful of boys. I couldn't avoid rolling my eyes at their satisfaction. I felt sorry for them, almost, for not having grown up just yet, and jealous too, for that very same thing.

"Earlier, were you looking at Marigold?" Ben said to me, whispering of course, so only I'd know what he's asking questions of. What dangerous inquiry kept reserved quiet for our very own controversy, looking back at it now. He was the bravest person I ever knew, untroubled by the consequence of finding my hand.

"I'm sorry," I said, looking briefly at him and then back to the bottle on the table. "I'd have no reason for doing that. You're crazy for thinking so."

"Oh, alright. I was just wondering."

And so he dropped it that easy, dismissing it from his mind the rest of the night, and the rest of his life.

"Who goes first!" Westley said. Casey was sitting beside him—sorry, first—did you make note yet that Ben was sat in between Marigold and me? It's just important you remember that significant detail of the story. You can ignore all other details so long as you confirm that one specially in writing and put it safe in the glass box above your bed, right by your Don Mattingly rookie card. Assuming you have that of course.

Anyway, Casey was beside Westley, wearing her scarf again and applying a new coat of soft pink lip gloss. Seeming to be excited to kiss a boy or girl that wasn't Westley for the first time in a while. I thought this was funny, and it got especially funnier when she offered to be first.

"OH!" Westley said. "Now that's my girl. You guys had better kiss her well."

He sent the bottle spinning. It made the noise of a spinning glass bottle admitting it's hollow, and got quiet and still at some boy I didn't know, and a boy Casey Morris certainly would never claim knowing. She looked disturbed by the bottle's choosing at random, but a game's a game, and you don't win getting the rules bent.

Standing carefully, Casey went over to the boy and kissed him, cutting a second in half. I noticed the boy extra red in the face when they finished, and Casey too—though she'd deny that forever if you ever mentioned it. On her way to sit back down beside Westley, she wiped her mouth with the backside of her hand, magnifying the performance to the fullest extent so everyone would notice and laugh. I felt so terrible for the boy that I had to close my eyes to get away. Ben elbowed me softly.

"Are you good?" he asked. I opened my eyes at his curiosity, seeing Casey leaning onto Westley's shoulder when I did, and feeling sick.

"Oh, yes. I'm fine," I told him, lying of course. I felt the world closing in.

"What are you guys talking for?" Westley said, gazing at me and Ben from across the room with the most awful sounding smile across his face. "Does one of you want to go next?"

"I don't think so," Ben said.

"Oh come on! Are you scared that you're a bad kisser!" Westley said.

"I'm not kissing anyone in front of my girlfriend."

"What about your boyfriend?" he asked insufferably, looking directly at me when he did. "Won't you kiss someone in front of him?"

"Don't start at all, Westley," Ben said, warning him it seemed from his sound of voice. I almost got scared myself, not having ever heard Ben speak that way before.

"Jesus. Don't go all psycho, Ben. I was joking. Since when do you take everything so fucking serious?"

"You don't get to—"

"Just spin the bottle already. I'll go next then," I said, interrupting them both. I didn't want a physical fight breaking out or anything. I don't know anyone who would have stopped that anyway. But not that it mattered in the very end—all this was so unimportant as the years ago.

"Damn right!" Westley said, officially sending the bottle into a spinning orbit arrangement, leaving my heartbeat to be guided by the necessary skipping process of the most awkward circumstance.

Even though I wasn't looking at him, I felt Ben's eyes fall onto me again, personally contemplating the landscape of my bravery. He pulled on the end of my shirt so to get my attention and read the new chapter's version I'd used the whole night reworking. It was the best thing I ever wrote and very fine writing also.

I looked at him.

"You'll get your chance for worrying about me later," I told him, blind to the particular fact that I'd be assuring him of that exact thing an hour later—except there'd be a fair amount of blood involved then, and no playing games. We had no knowledge of the time ahead yet.

I heard the bottle stop spinning. I sat forward to find its landing place, and my eyes joined the eyes of this girl with bright yellow hair. She was pretty, I remember, and wearing lots of face makeup. She looked nothing like Maisie, I thought, and then I was thinking about how Maisie would behave discovering I'd kissed a girl who resembled absolutely no part of her. Would she hate me forever—or forgive me in time, well, the next time she was eager to play with my hands. But my worrying efforts had no meaning—unnecessary, I found, to even begin worrying. Worse things were advancing through the wind of the night, passing through the trees, influencing. Don't mind the knocking at the window! It's just the wind making you afraid.

I got up and went over to the bright yellow haired girl. She was smiling at me a pretty exterior, risky expulsion of a love affair.

"You have a cut on your lip," she said.

"I know," I said. I don't get why people point out things you left the mirror noticing.

"Is that going to hurt?"

"I don't know, maybe."

"Have you ever kissed a girl before?" she asked.

"Have you ever kissed a boy before?" I said, returning the same mocking remark in a much better envelope, making everyone laugh when I did. I would never be so mean to a girl on a typical day, but I had White Lightning following the passageway of veins up to my brain, conducting acid green poisoning.

"You have a lame brain," she said back in this very sober manner that seemed goddamn impolite and quite worse than my demeanor prior. I regret ever kissing her, and I know it was only a game, but there was a frequency of stage whispering that had absolutely nothing to do with the amusement of bottle spinning.

"Kiss already!" I heard someone in the audience say. And so we kissed, in colorless regard of course, having no inspired phrases to come from it. I'd never kissed a girl with bright yellow spiraling hair before and I don't have much interest in doing that again.

There was clapping from everyone and I felt stupid, common and factory made. I never stopped feeling that way since.

When I sat back down, Ben said, "You don't seem yourself."

"I don't know why you'd say that. I'm the best I've ever felt," I told him.

"Your eyes are big."

"Why's that bothering you?" I asked.

"I'm just worrying about you."

"Oh, well, of course you are. That's all you ever do apparently."

"You're being mean," he said. He couldn't have known there was some terrible and cute, white veiled, baby angel speaking very bad things in my left ear about everyone in that room. I wonder, really, if this was the first time I ever felt absolutely mad. There was a well-lit golden ceiling fixture, though, and I've always believed fluorescents can do that—make you feel absolutely mad. So maybe it was just the lighting equipment needed adjusting.

"Is that disappointing?" I said.

"I mean, a little bit, yes. You're always the nicest person."

"Oh, well, yes, yes, how tragic. I've changed with the night."

"You're not making any sense."

"Has it taken you this long to notice?" I asked.

"Jack, that's not all of it—" he began saying but of course Westley interrupted again, asking who was going next. It was surprising just how quickly Marigold's hand went up. Her hair was dripping wet still, from the pool, and onto her light pink tee shirt, making obvious the red inner coating.

"Marigold Adams!" Westley said, incapable of ever keeping excitement private. "What would your mother think!" He laughed at himself.

"What are you up to?" she said to him. It was the first time I ever saw her decently annoyed, rolling her eyes at him. "Can't you spin the bottle?"

"Fine, fine," he said, absolutely dissatisfied by her reluctance to participate in his teasing. I smiled in the midst of all the delight, glad to watch his kingship fall off little by little—unhurried, yes, but falling anyhow.

Westley let the bottle go, rotating about the table how a spin top would. I studied Ben's eyes moving seconds on a clock hand, just as though he was getting ready for the hour nearby. And it would be such a long hour—the longest of my life. I believe someone was in the drawing room, in the dark most certainly, moving past the lines and drawing minutes out into weeks.

He wasn't breathing any. It seemed that he was putting off that task for when the bottle paused on somebody, but when it did finally stop, he still didn't exhale or anything. Breathing was impossible muscle behavior when the bottle had found the worst stopping point on me. I wondered, honestly, if Westley's hand movement was talented enough to blame—or if fate was the misdoing once again, ruining every category of anything at all. The whole grand amount of thrill passed.

My heart sank immediately, burying itself next to my favorite dead, and letting dust get all over it at the floor's basis. I couldn't find a golden dustpan close by for dusting it off—necessary of the golden quality for also cleaning up the broken glass filings later on.

"How likely is that!" Westley said, smiling at his own trouble making. Was the evening designed by him and his troubled mind? Did I hear him out on the roof earlier, coloring the sky nighttime, intensifying the mischief profile of horizontal lines? I was stupid and blind, unobserving with a very distracted mind. But anyway, there's not anything I can do about it now.

"Marigold and Jack!" Casey spoke for the first time again since kissing that awful looking boy from before. I wished she'd go completely quiet if forever. "Who would have ever thought?"

I glanced at Ben, looking for his opinion on the whole thing, but his face seemed clean, blank of any poetic meaning. I should have taken that as part of an early warning sign—the traffic symbol of a new life. But I was too stupid and blind, I've told you already, unobserving with a very distracted mind.

"I'm not doing that, sorry," I said.

"Oh, relax, Jack! It's a game. It doesn't have to mean anything," Casey said, speaking yet again, even though no one asked for her noisy way of thinking.

"I don't mind kissing you, Jack," Marigold said, apparently unmoved by Ben's possible sensitivity to it all. "I have to say I find your hesitancy a little offensive, honestly."

"You have a boyfriend, and he's sitting right there," I said, nodding at Ben. I felt uncomfortable that Marigold was pressing for this, and I expect he felt the same way, despite his straight face.

"And you have a girlfriend! Does that make your kissing endeavors any better?"

"It's fine!" Ben said, abruptly cutting in. "It's just a game anyway. Doesn't hold any significance at all."

"Yes, exactly, Ben!" Westley said. "Don't keep everyone waiting the whole night. Some of us would like to keep playing."

I looked at Ben again, this time trying to solve his inexpressive calculation, but I couldn't attain any bit of understanding. I'd known him my whole life—had kissing him unraveled all that previous wisdom? My line of thought was totally out of shape, impulse wiring cables entangled.

Marigold's eyes confronted mine, burning the sockets inside into twelve little business fires, clearing out any good sense I had left in my brain, it seemed. And then we kissed right in front of Ben, in the truest sense those words could ever offer. Remember, a few pages before, how I told you he sat in between the two of us?

Marigold leaned over him, with all her strength, to grab my shirt's collar and pull me towards her. I'd never kissed Marigold, and so I don't know what I expected, but it wasn't anything like I would have ever imagined. She has a very nice, gentle technique about it, while also hurrying the process through its clumsiness. I'd never kissed a girl that way—in fact the only person I'd kissed that same way was Ben! Were they imitating each other? Is the art of kissing so easy and achieved by little meaning?

It was a big relief when she pulled away—not because I didn't enjoy kissing her, but the very opposite. I found the corners of my mouth enjoyed it far too much—the dangerous breathtaking cliffs that would eventually convince me to jump from them if I didn't know any better otherwise.

After, she let go of my shirt collar, and I haunted my mind with every consequence possible—except one that I would have never thought of, not if I were offered all the gold currency in the world. Even today I sometimes don't believe it still. I know Ben is below the wet ground, and he designed his name better forgotten about, but I don't believe it still. He's just gone for the long weekend vacation, visiting family in a different place. He's coming back on Monday—he told me so himself—and we'll go swimming. He would never leave me all on my own in this stupid, big world when he knows I am most afraid of staying behind anyway. Maybe he's just walking home and that's what taking him so very long to get home.

Sometimes getting home can be the worst thing you ever do, if it's dark especially, and the paper boy is also on his way home, too, and you can't see him in enough time. Is there ever enough time?

They all kept playing the game, requiring lots of more kissing and difficulty breathing. I sat there uncertain of the close property I'd spent many years of my whole life making—picking out favorite wall paintings, colors for the carpets and decorating the mailbox with garland string. Had I broken nearly everything I could or was there more ready and waiting? I miss having a simple mind and cool, innocent eyes.

Eventually, though, the game was over and the music was noisy again and people were dancing again. My visible horizon got all blurry, and my shoes were no longer on my feet. I don't know where I put them, and I don't remember taking them off, but I didn't have them at this point. The policeman was very curious about this so I thought I'd make note of it.

"I don't feel very well, at all," I said to Ben. I'd let the uncertainty get so far to my head it was tying shoelaces around my brain and double knotting them in a contest of best knots.

"Do you want to leave?" he asked. I told him yes. "I just have to find Marigold first and say goodbye, if that's alright. Don't move from this spot."

He disappeared for a long matter of seconds. I couldn't get the shoelaces undone in his length of absence because a new danger was introduced—my heart was getting chased now by a killer and the masquerade dance he came from looked to be a magnificent one, layered with money and expensive benefits. Madness was going around and the carousel was not dropping anyone off. You would have to jump if you sought escape, though you'd break every little bone in your dead body, incomparable to that time on the park swing. In my greatest estimation, you'd feel it a whole decade later still, and it would burn the new curtains you've just hung. And when you were listening for the songbirds, you forgot to close the window and the killer broke in while you weren't home so all that running you did forever ago was useless. In the end you realize nothing's ever so important but the lovely end.

But anyway, Ben came back again.

"Did you find Marigold?" I asked.

"I did," he said. "She's staying for a little while longer. I told her you weren't feeling well and so I'm taking you home. No throwing up in my car, though, please. My dad would absolutely kill me."

"I'll try my goddamn, truest best."

"I'd appreciate that, thank you."

And so we left Westley's house, and that very brief life behind. We wandered a couple of streets over to Ben's car.

"Is it midnight already?" I asked. I noticed the streetlamps were on, glaring a brightly colored yellow in a higher light than regular. If you're ever in Cradock, you'll find they only do this in the very dark, dead of night when no one's playing outside. It's the best and worst time harmonizing at the same time.

"What makes you think so?" Ben asked.

"The streetlamps are giving it away."

"Hm. I've never paid much attention to that," he said.

We let the varying levels of gravel after Harwich Boulevard be a time consuming process, very quiet in that, and I suppose it's especially good we did because these were the last moments we'd ever find ourselves together. It's not too long before everything loses color and favorite patterns go absolutely dull forever. I have tried sharpening them many times over again since but I can't ever seem to get the pocket knife angled just right, and my hands often get cut trying. I've dealt with enough blood this lifetime and there's nothing at all worth such a high value accessory anymore.

I tapped my fingers on the passenger door handle in a rapid pace, waiting for Ben to finally unlock the car. I really wanted to go home, I remember. I was feeling so awfully blue and not only that, but I had the worst headache of my whole life.

"Do you love me, right?" I asked Ben.

"Most of the time," he said.

"I don't know what that means."

"You don't have to know everything."

"Oh, well, I want to."

He unlocked the car and we both got inside.

Almost immediately, in Ben's car, we were ourselves again at our goddamn, truest best and my eyesight was certain again about suffering from a great distance.

"Do you want the radio on?" Ben asked nicely.

"No, thanks, that's fine," I said, lying my head back on the headrest and staring out the front glass. "I have the worst headache of my whole life. Could you make the air cold, though? I'm warm."

"Don't be a wise guy."

"I can't ever help it."

"Are you wearing the seatbelt?" he asked.

"I happen to be putting it on right now," I said, doing exactly that. He wouldn't ever drive anywhere if you didn't have the seatbelt on first. His discretion was always wide and kind, going far enough outside the city line, but in the end an ordinary, terrifically, powerless thing. Life's a small kid's taunting device.

He started driving us home—almost soundless except the heartbeat disturbance in my head and the air ventilation doing its best. I was very eager to get home, but Ben didn't seem that way. I don't remember him going very fast at all, and so you might not understand how any of this happened. Would you ever believe if I told you the road was improper enough already, wet from the brief rainstorm earlier? Maybe that's how everything got all bent out of very perfect shape. In private for many weeks after, at night beneath my bed's special covering only, I blamed the gravel's bad language. I kept this excuse balanced upright on the flat tip of my finger for the longest time. I trimmed my nails in accordance, and painted them a silvery gray. But then someday eventually, I forgot, and made a promise with that same finger, and all of the changes and blame gave way in big waves and I developed admiration in a different idea. I sat by the window in the daytime, and bathed in the brightness of the daylight.

We were passing Harwich Boulevard, I remember. I was staring out the side window, having a dim suspicion of broken road signs.

"Westley must've hit the stop sign again. I don't know how you miss that," I said, exposing curiosity in Ben's mind of course. I should have known that would happen anyway. His focus was always a different thing—maybe the worst thing about him if I ever had to decide. He looked over at the sign, putting the avenue ahead in blind knowledge, and I looked forward at the worst possible time.

There was a boy crossing the street on his bike—I'd later find out this was the newest paperboy, finalizing memory of his route before the next morning. I screamed at Ben to stop, and the abrupt focus recovery must have frightened him so bad because he sent the car spinning out. I felt everything pause for a moment, and I saw a very bright fluorescent demonstration of my life story, and it was not a very good one.

Spinning out, Ben tried avoiding the paperboy, but simply missed. After we hit a very big tree. I woke up covered in the broken windshield glass. I looked over at Ben absolutely dying. He had his eyes shut, and there was blood on every part of clothing he wore. I moved instantly to get out of my seatbelt, at first struggling to get it unfixed. My hands were shaking.

I said his name, and his eyes fluttered tiny little butterfly wings. I sighed crazy relief, and started crying.

"Are you safe?" he asked. I heard his voice quality break.

"I'm safe. Don't worry about that," I said. "I just have to get your seatbelt undone. Can you move?"

"I didn't see the boy," he said. "Did I kill him?"

"I don't know, but don't worry about that. Can you move at all?"

"I probably killed him, Jack."

"Oh, goddamn it, Ben, can you move!!!" I was really crying now, and so was he. He started repeating how sorry he was over again as though it would ever bring the paperboy back to life. "Please stop that! You didn't do anything bad!"

"My dad's going to kill me," he said.

"I won't let him get near you," I said. My hands relaxed enough that I finally got him out of his seatbelt, and when I did, that's when I saw this big piece of glass in his waistline. It seemed deep from the blood running from it. I never saw blood ever that dark red in my whole life and I didn't know how to stop it. I could save him, but I could never save him enough. My brain went completely numb, and I must have shown it on my face. We both knew opportunity was at the end. There would be no new life.

"Can I live at your house with you?" he said.

"I have to ask my dad permission first," I told him, trying to soften conversation. "He likes you enough to say yes."

"I'm glad. You'll have to let him know I said thanks about that."

"Right away."

"And let Marigold know she's pretty. She never believes me when I say that. Maybe she'll believe you." I couldn't stop crying once he said that, and he laughed. I saw blood all throughout his pretty white teeth when he did. "Why are you crying?"

"It's not important," I said. "What should we do tomorrow?"

"I have chores tomorrow."

"What about the next day?"

"I could probably do something. I'll call you."

"I'll look forward to it the whole day," I said.

"Boring day," he said.

"Just a normal day, really."

"Do you mind if I just rest my eyes?" he said. "I'm kind of tired."

"Oh, that's fine. I love you," I said.

"I love you more," he said, shutting his eyes forever. I listened only to him breathing for a little while, until he wasn't breathing any.

I let myself cry. And then I climbed out of the car through the broken windshield. I let glass get in my hands and my bare feet, too. Outside, there was glass everywhere. I thought the sky might have fallen. I saw the paperboy lying dead in the middle of the street. I walked over to his body, felt his wrist for any bit of life, and felt nothing.

I started running fast. I ran all the way to the police station and I told the first policeman I saw everything. He seemed most worried about my feet, though, and the blood at my heels. But then a nice lady came from behind the reception desk and hugged me extra close. I started crying again and I didn't stop for days, leaving my eyes cherry red—almost exactly how they were in the bathroom mirror at Macauley from the dust particle I'd retrieved. Do you remember the beginning?

Ansel was calling my name, saving me from further memory.

"What do you need?" I asked.

"I can't get this button off," he said. I wiped my eyes of the current bearing the suffering past and came from the bathroom. He was finally taking off my coat I'd given him—or trying to, I mean, anyway. He would have taken a whole lifetime if I wasn't there probably. I always wonder how different our lives would be having never met. I'm still learning plenty.

He couldn't figure out the top button, I remember, and there was a quiet voice choir telling bitter jokes of coincidental things always happening. Ansel got upset so easy, and he was becoming very angry at the button. You couldn't interrupt him at these present moments— well, you could if you really wanted, yes, but that would be a horrible defense and a lot harder to get him quiet after. I always left him to his angry self when he got that way. I'd go and read a magazine of second draft poems instead, or dream about a completely new life.

He tore the button clean off the jacket and disposed of it on the wood floor.

"Did you really have to tear it apart?" I asked him. "It was barely yours."

"I'm sorry. Did you want it back some day?" he asked.

I told him I wasn't very interested.

I saw Maisie often. Every morning I'd meet her in the common room for a different card game entertainment. We could play for hours without disturbance, except maybe, if by accident, my eyes stalled on her pretty face yet another time and improper things formed in my mind. I never slept in a bed with Maisie, though. I only ever kissed her a lot of times. I don't know if I regret this or not, or if I like knowing Maisie the way I did—young and alive.

One day, Ansel asked where I was going "every goddamn morning" and "so early at that."

"I'm playing cards," I told him.

"Oh, all by yourself?" he asked, entertaining himself apparently. "I know you're with that girl. Why haven't I met her yet?"

"I don't know," I said. "I don't think you'd get along that well anyway." I knew differently, actually, that they'd be the best of friends—and possibly something more terrible. I couldn't threaten everything I knew introducing them both, but I could only keep them apart so long.

"I should know your girlfriend, though," he said. "I know every other thing about you."

"She's not my girlfriend, and no, you don't. What always makes you think that?"

"I hear you dream," he said. I got a little scared because I knew he really meant that.

But anyway, Ansel did meet Maisie one day, and it went how I expected, and the work between them progressed quickly. It was by January they were absolutely fascinated by each other. Even the smallest things they did together, for example, solving crossword puzzles and putting up holiday decorations in the dining hall. Maisie could be found often laying in Ansel's cot, suntanning in a fleece nightgown at your first glance, while only being confused by the bedding's thin white clothes. And just so you know, I didn't mind any bit of their going out. I was never dating Maisie ever anyway, though I had definitely loved her at some point. But I didn't love her that way anymore. I stopped loving that way a while ago.

One time, though, Ansel did ask my opinion on the whole love affair. "Do you mind?" he asked.

"Not ever," I told him. And I really meant that, despite my known performance history of hard feelings. Wasn't it a new life anyway?

We made it through the winter. It was cold and difficult most of the time, killing all of the leaves too. I was glad to have Ansel and Maisie both in Macauley together at once. I don't know how I would've survived otherwise. My dad came to visit on Christmas day. I didn't ask for anything but he got me a new baseball hat anyway. After he left that day, I had hot drinking chocolate with Ansel and Maisie and we exchanged our self-made gift attempts. I gave Ansel a paper airplane bent with special craft paper I'd found in the drawing room. He gave me the button he tore from my jacket. I wrote a poem for Maisie, and she drew a portrait of me. I have the drawing still, folded up in my desk drawer. It was the best Christmas I ever had yet.

I found time passing absolutely fine. Regularly, that would've bothered me to some very great extent, but if I had let every small thing upset me in my days at Macauley, I would have gone totally mad. I was certain Ansel and Maisie felt the same way I did, but among just themselves, while I watched the reflection of everyone dancing, they must have designed their running away together.

It was a February morning and the first warm day of the year we'd gotten. So warm enough to prop open every window at home and leave the curtains dancing all by themselves. At Macauley though, and I've mentioned this before, the windows don't open all the way. You can only get them about a hand's length up. Ansel said that was so nobody could jump out, but for some reason, the window opens completely in the drawing room. Ansel told me about that, too, before I knew anything at all.

And so the staff opened the windows that day, just enough as they could try, and the warm air swept through every corridor, yes, but you found it warmest in the drawing room, where the drawing paper danced so much at the window's new character degree.

That next morning, I was woken up by Ansel shaking me awake, telling me they couldn't find Maisie.

"What time is it even?" I asked, blinking myself just barely awake. I don't like waking up very early at all. "Is it early in the morning?"

"It's almost seven," he said. "They're waking everyone. They can't find her anywhere."

"What do you mean?" I said, getting up out of bed—fully awake at the detail. "She couldn't have gone anywhere."

"I don't really know what's going on," he said. I saw him nervous in his hand movement. "I just came to get you. They're gathering a crowd in the dining hall."

I put my shoes on fast as ever and we met everyone in the chaos of the dining hall. In the very turbulent madness, crowd of about forty people, the orderlies tried to get everyone quiet. Once they succeeded in that effort, they formally declared the matter of Ansel's nervous hands.

Maisie Kenton was missing.

And I don't have any good news about that.

She isn't found still.

<u>Chapter 9</u>:

The Tragedy of Growing Up Forever

Phoebe came to my house the other day. It was raining too heavy outside for me to ride my bike to Paton Street, and too cold also. Have you felt the small change in weather? I noticed it on my way home from school first—the leaves taunting the coolest boys, whistling. It must be September already.

Anyway, she decided to come visit me at home instead. It was strange. I've only ever known her to exist in her tiny, violet office. Seeing her in a different place was absolutely bizarre, and every remark felt I was playing pretend. I couldn't stop it, really. I don't know how to behave out of the ordinary.

She read through a couple of pages in my journal. She didn't say much at all about it. Her quiet attitude sent my nerves running in the shadows of excessive thinking. I heard my dad on the phone with her later that night. I couldn't hear anything too well, though. For some reason they were whispering. But nothing has come of that just yet. How long do I wait? Do I keep the fire burning anyway?

I see Marigold everyday now. Finding her at my doorstep again was like putting on the oldest pullover I have and learning it fits still. She's the very same as before, and so am I, mostly, except the number of sufferings that bleed through the expensive room set table napkins once a day. I really do my best to forget them, while Marigold does better at understanding them. She has the most intelligent observations. I find myself waiting by the door all the time.

We spend time outside often. Just yesterday we were at the park and we sat on the swings for a little while.

"Did you know I broke my arm falling off these?" I said.

"Was that long ago?" she asked.

"Sometime when I was a lot smaller and had way brittle bones."

"Don't you have them anymore?"

"No, well—I don't know," I said. "How am I supposed to know?"

"What are you feeling right now?" she asked.

"Not anything too specific, really."

"Oh, well, I can't help you much with that. I can help you get home, though."

"I know my way home well enough, but thanks for offering anyway."

I gave the Earth a playful little push with my foot, setting my swing just barely moving.

"Jack, could I ask you something?" Marigold said.

"Anything that you need," I said.

She let everything go still—even the wind ceased activity for a moment, I swear, and somewhere in New

York City a taxi cabdriver won't move at the green light. No one's going anywhere.

"Did Ben die right away?" she said. "I know you guys hit the tree, but did he die at that moment, or was there a certain amount of time that he was suffering?"

I gave myself a minute to answer. The taximen finally going.

"He was happy to the very end," I told her. I've told myself that anyway.

Marigold and I have made a routine of going to the bookshop every Wednesday, but today she was busy at home doing kitchen chores. I think my dad felt bad I'd have to go alone because he gave me twenty dollars to spend this time when usually he gives me only ten, and so I was able to get two books. I was putting the money I didn't use in my wallet when I heard this girl's voice I knew. I looked up to find the girl with the red hair that I've told you about before. I haven't mentioned it yet, but her name is Margot Klous. She told me that a little while ago in the front office when I was leaving school. I just didn't have any good reason to write it down until today.

"Hey, Margot," I said once I saw her.

"Oh, hey, Jack," she said. "All by yourself today?"

"What do you mean?" I asked.

"Aren't you with Marigold usually?" she said.

"She was busy today. Do you always pay that much attention?"

"Am I not supposed to?"

"Oh, not at all. You should close your eyes when you drive."

She laughed, quite loud as a fire alarm would laugh, but it wasn't even so good of a joke to inspire that kind of amusing housefire. Did you think so anyway?

"Do you have someplace to be?" she asked. She was giving me a deep stare by use of her green eyes. I didn't feel at all frightened, though.

"No, I just have to get home by six," I said.

"That's fine. Can I show you something?"

"I know everywhere already. I've lived here my whole life so far."

There was a tiny pause, letting the small hanging bells of the door frame play at new shopper's arriving. Margot was smiling very significantly at me—happy as Maisie did at every card game win.

"I promise you can't have known this place yet," she said.

"I don't believe that very much at all."

"It has security. Big, black dogs at the fence, and you can't get by them, so you couldn't have ever gone there."

"Oh, well, how could you have?"

"Because I've lived there my whole life so far," she said, glowing in a way that exposed the tragedy of growing up forever in the same place had not once bothered her at any time before. She sighed at my not understanding apparently. "I'm inviting you over."

"I don't know you very well, though," I told her.

"We have all day for getting to know each other very well," she said.

For just a moment I thought the offer over, contemplating the uncertainty of all safety devices if I followed this girl home. My heart beat every different misgiving at top volume the very thought of everything.

I covered the first page of suggestion, pacing myself for growing old later, and slipped on the carousel writing prose.

She lives on Angeles Street in the only blue house I've ever known. It's one story tall, and has a fence bordering the whole front yard perimeter. I noticed the grass also not cut recently at all.

We were greeted outside by two dogs barking. They were big as she described them, but not so threatening in behavior up close. "Did you ever have a dog?" Margot asked, bending her knees to pet them both at their ears.

"Once, when I was a lot younger," I said. "His name was Russ."

"That's a very cute name. What's it from?"

"Oh, I don't know. My mom thought of it. What have you named them?"

"Alex and Finnegan," she said. "You're welcome to pet them. They've never bitten anyone."

And so I bent down on my knees as well, and pet them both at their ears. They were very soft.

Margot had a housekey in the small area of her front pocket that she used to open the door. I followed her in, the first piece of floorboard creaking at my steps, gleaming at the shape of a new stranger's presence when I did. "I don't normally have people over," she said.

Inside wasn't at all how I would have expected. It was nearly empty of house belongings, as though no one was actually living there, but a little red, wooden piano in the corner.

"Where are your things?" I asked.

"I don't have very much," she said. "Just what I need."

She made her way over to the piano, sitting down on the red velvet cushioning when she got there. She closed her eyes and played a few notes out of memory and sight. I knew them right away. I got dizzy at the recognition, falling to my side in a bad rush of frequency. I started over at the beginning in the most recent place of dancing.

I was in Macauley again.

I heard Phoebe's voice coming from the dark offstage. "How long was he sleeping for?" she said.

"Not that long," somebody responded. I didn't know that voice anywhere.

"Has he opened his eyes at all yet?" Phoebe asked.

I hadn't. It didn't have anything to do with not being able to. I just didn't want to look at anybody's goddamn face. I find listening much better anyway.

"Is that so necessary?" I said, not opening my eyes yet still.

"Don't be difficult, Jack, please," Phoebe said, and so I opened them that very moment. You could feel everyplace on my body and discover asking me nicely is my weakest spot.

"What time is it?" I asked, blinking as though creek water was all in my eyes. I was realizing my eyesight was kind of blurry.

"Oh, that's not very important right now, Jack," Phoebe said. She didn't sound herself all of a sudden, but rather a much older, quieter lady deeming great relevance. "It's only important that you're safe."

"What do you mean?" I asked.

"You were in a housefire," she said. I sat up instantly. I didn't remember anything about a housefire.

"I don't believe so. I would know if that happened of course. What are you doing?"

"Jack, relax, please," Phoebe said. I felt my heart racing and my face reddening all over. "It's important that you stay relaxed."

"But what about Margot?"

"Who's that?"

"I was at Margot's house, wasn't I?"

"No, you were at home alone, Jack. Who's Margot?"

I was blinking at the same pace of my heartbeat—a rapid game of coin toss flipping and winning guarantee. I didn't quite know what was going on, apparently.

"How did a fire start?" I asked.

"Your heart's too big."

"But how's that?" I said. It didn't make any good sense.

"You must be falling in love again," she said.

I woke up from the worst nightmare I ever had. I went downstairs to get a drink of water, and listened for any songbirds as the faucet ran. I didn't hear anything but the months whispering time away. I tapped my finger on the countertop in rhythm of the beating in my head, finishing off my water glass while I did that. I decided I had better sleep again. I find each day in need of more energy than already before, and the tragedy of growing up forever awfully boring. Should it require a whole chapter anyway?

I remember the morning of picture day at school in the second grade, using sewing scissors to cut my own hair. It came out a horrible looking mess that my mom was just barely able to fix, but she somehow managed anyway.

All throughout my mom's chemotherapy treatment, my mom's hair would fall out in every place. It was very hard for her to get used to, and so eventually she just cut all her hair off. When she did that, she showed me these school photographs of when she was a little girl with short, boy's hair.

"I look that same way again," she said, laughing.

Chapter 10:

The Boy and the Horseshoe

Cradock, PA—GIRL FOUND NEAR RAILWAY TRACKS

"Do they know who she was?" Margot asked regarding today's newspaper headline. It was delivered to my front door early today.

"No, they haven't released the girl's name yet," I said. "In motion train strikes girl late Sunday night at about ten fifteen o'clock near Seamus Junction. She was found by switch operator, Henry Carlton, who was at work on the eastbound tracks."

Margot and I were sitting on my bedroom floor, listening to my clock radio. She came by my house this morning, bringing the paper inside when she did.

"Could it be somebody from school?" she said.

"I don't know, maybe," I said. "I wouldn't like to think so anyway. They wrote that she's at Saint Sacred Heart Hospital recovering."

I pulled at the wool of my sweater in nervous energy. I couldn't avoid thinking the girl could be Maisie Kenton, but it couldn't be! Absolutely not. She'd notice an onrushing train, wouldn't she?

"What are you thinking?" Margot asked. "That it's Maisie Kenton?"

"Maybe that's why they haven't said any name just yet," I said. "Her parents don't want anything revealed—"

"—Jack, stop. You're ruining the cuff on your sweater," Margot said. I stopped pulling at the wool following her demand.

"Oh, I hadn't noticed."

Downstairs, the housephone began to ring. Immediately, I got up and ran to it. Marigold was on the other end.

"Hey, Jack," she said. She was talking a little quiet, as though a bug at my window. "Are you busy right now?"

I told her I wasn't, answering that I had the whole day to myself if I wanted.

"I'm going to come by your house," she said.

"Oh, well, I'm not dressed or anything yet. I had better take a shower first."

"I think you'll find that's not very important," she said. I had a very bad feeling all of a sudden. I couldn't think of any good reason she'd have to say that.

I waited by the door for her to arrive, resuming practice of pulling on my sweater while I did. Marigold's dad is the editor at the Cradock Post if you forgot already, and so he might know the girl in the headline. I felt nervous as my shaking hands were.

"What's happening?" Margot asked, standing from the top of the staircase. I'd forgotten she was at my house. How did she get there anyway?

"Marigold is coming over," I said.

"Is that why you look very nervous?" she said, coming down the stairs. Her blouse varying colors at each step, bright and dim infinite rosy grin. I knew I was dreaming of course, from any dream I ever had before, but also when a bag of marbles fell from the ceiling—a storm of partly colored gumdrops beside me.

I woke up to the telephone ringing. It was Marigold.

"Did I wake you up?" she asked. "I know it's early."

"No, you didn't," I said, lying away the daylight already. I have to get better at stopping that. "I got up a little while ago. I couldn't sleep very well."

"Oh, I'm sorry. Are you busy today?"

"I don't think so. I didn't plan anything necessarily."

I looked down at the sweater I slept in, noticing right away threads coming apart as if they were disruptive leaves growing in expensive grass. But pulling at them, wasn't that a dream?

"Have you read today's newspaper?" she asked. I felt my heart stop for a moment again. Everything felt terrifically devised just as though I were dreaming still.

"I haven't yet," I said. "Was it delivered already?"

"Oh, yes—Jack, I don't know how to say this—" Her words tangled amongst themselves in double knots. "Oh, Jack—" she said again, "Casey Morris is dead."

"What, how?" I asked. My heartbeat was speeding up, grieving easy behavior. I couldn't believe it.

"Westley shot her yesterday, and himself, too. In front of everybody at church service."

I lowered the telephone, pulling on the chord as I moved a little closer to the kitchen window. For the first time in a really long time, I swore that I could hear them—the songbirds—and they were in echoing chorus Ansel interrogating me before. "Do you think it's a mad world?" he said, and they were saying it over and over again in seamless coordination.

Marigold spoke faintly through the phone. I brought it back up to my ear, dismissing the songbirds calling. It wasn't happening—it was all in my head. Remind yourself that and don't let it happen again.

"It was so horrible, Jack. Both of their parents were there."

"Were you there?" I asked, worrying she had the best sitting place for another group suffering.

"Oh, no, I was at home yesterday morning doing homework for Mr. Levings, thank goodness. Have you started the homework yet?"

"No, I haven't. Do you think we'll have school tomorrow anyway?" I asked. We had the past three days off for an extended weekend vacation because of water pipes leaking and ruining the ceiling access panels.

"School's not canceled, at least not yet," she said. "They're having a candlelight vigil later tonight. I wanted to ask you first if you might like to go. They were both our classmates."

"Where are they having it?" She didn't say anything at first. I had to repeat myself. She sighed.

"At Westley's house," she said. "His parents are organizing the whole thing. Don't you think they must feel awful?"

"I'm surprised they're home, honestly. I wouldn't have expected that from them," I said. Westley's parents were absent constantly.

"Jack, please don't talk that way right now," Marigold said. "It's upsetting." I could hear her voice shaking—dimming the lights brightened. I felt a little scared, and terrible for speaking so openly.

"I'm sorry," I told her. I really meant it, too. "What time is the vigil?"

"Eight o'clock," she said. "I'll pick you up twenty minutes before then."

"Certainly," I said. I set the phone hanging after, and right as I did, it began to ring again. I picked the phone back up.

"Who's this?" I asked.

"Is that how you start all your telephone calls?" a boy's voice said. I recognized the voice even before he finished talking. I just couldn't believe myself at first, and I'm very afraid you might not believe me either. But I've only lied once yet.

The voice was Ansel.

"How did you—" I began to say, but I couldn't seem to get a proper sentence going long enough that meant anything. I let the counter top bear all of my body's weight. Falling against it was my only safety.

"You sound pretty as ever, barely able to put a whole sentence together," Ansel said. "What are you doing now?"

"How did you get my house's phone number?" I said straightly, replacing my surprise for my displeasure. I couldn't believe him and his late promptness calling. I'd spent months wondering about him. I could have spent my whole life if necessary.

"Maisie's got it by heart," he said. "She doesn't forget hardly anything. I was going to remember it eventually."

"Ansel, honestly, what the fuck are you doing?" I shifted focus to my breathing, holding and letting go when it became essential. My throat was burning in the freezing cold—burning a candle in the winter storm.

September was over a while ago.

"I'm just wondering how you were," Ansel said. His voice was innocent against mine, and I felt so terrible yelling at him the way I did. I couldn't stop myself crying.

And then came a different voice over the line saying my name—nice, lovely and music box deserving. I'd spent many nights dreaming this moment to the very point beyond abstract imagination, almost forgetting what the real world even looked like in the daytime. Knowing she was alive was plenty enough relief to live a whole decade of—just not forever.

I let it go completely quiet, holding my breath even.

"Jack, are you there?" Maisie Kenton asked. "Ansel said you went quiet. I didn't believe that, though. For all the years I've known you, you haven't quit talking once."

I could only hold my breath so long.

"Did you ever expect it would be alright?" I said. My eyes were going blind from the crying.

"I'm going to be very honest, Jack. I don't know if you'll like that any," Maisie said. My heart was gathering speed, hurrying quivering. "First, you have to stop crying. However are you going to hear me otherwise?"

I gave it my best to stop, drafting strategy noiselessly. Maisie waited quietly.

Then she exhaled greatly.

"We've known each other a good amount of time, Jack, and your heart's very big and you're very caring and you listen the most of any boy I've ever met, but it got to be too much. I don't know how to handle that kind of thing. I had to get away before I let any of it affect you somehow. I couldn't help feeling wasteful."

"You never had to save me," I said.

"I never was trying to save you, Jack. I was saving myself most of all. Do you realize that?"

"I would have done the same."

"No, you wouldn't have, Jack. You're a good man."

I sighed. She was always a great conversationalist.

"Where are you living?" I asked.

"I'm in Washington at my aunt's house," she said.

"Do your parents know that?" She didn't answer right away.

"I didn't want you coming after me, Jack. I asked them to not let you know."

"Does Marigold know?"

"I haven't spoken to Marigold since days before I went to Macauley. She doesn't know anything."

"She's your best friend, though. You should have told her anyway."

"I can't do that."

"Why not? She always wonders if I know anything about where you are."

"I don't know what I'd say to her. She would never understand. It's easier if I just leave you two alone."

"Don't you find that unfair? She doesn't even know if you're alive." She started crying.

"I'm sorry, Jack, but I can't do anything further. It was difficult enough calling you already."

"What reason did you call anyway?"

"Ansel's going home," she said. "He's leaving this afternoon."

"What do you mean?" I couldn't seem to understand what she meant—I don't know why, when it was a very simple message. Ansel was coming home. I would see him later today.

"Are you able to meet him at the bus station? He's going to need someplace to stay as well."

I stared intently at the walls to be certain they weren't misshapen and that I wasn't dreaming. They didn't bend at all.

"He should get there about six o'clock," Maisie said. "We're packing his things. He doesn't have very much. Are you able to meet him? I don't want him to arrive and no one's expecting him."

"I'll get him," I said. I had stopped crying completely by this point from the eagerness of seeing my friend again.

She sighed relief. "I really appreciate that, Jack."

"I know," I said.

"I miss you very much," she said. I could have started crying again.

"You can always come back anytime you want."

"Oh, no, I couldn't ever interfere. Besides, I'm busy as the day."

"That's too bad. I could always use you."

"No, you couldn't. You're doing just fine, whether or not you've realized it yet." She paused, taking a step backwards in her dressiest business fabrics, toe dancing in black leg covering pantyhose—the only attire fit for the moment. In the brief silence, I had barely enough time to process the curtains being drawn. For just a second the room grew entirely dark—the window's view speechless in the occasion. Breathing in deeply, and breathing out the same way, you could hear the uncertainty in my exhaling quite easily from a mile off, if you were paying any small attention to the wind today.

We were saying goodbye.

"I got very lucky meeting you, Jack Boyd. It was so wonderful getting to know you," she said.

"Don't be a stranger, Maisie Kenton."

"Oh, well, that couldn't ever happen. You know me too well enough."

"I'll love you forever," I said.

"I hope that you do," she said. "Goodbye, Jack."

I didn't officially say goodbye. I just breathed again, and when she gave the phone over to Ansel, I told him I'd meet him at the bus station later that night. His smile beamed through the phone, and I swore he almost broke the whole thing.

"Is it snowing there?" he asked.

"What? No, it's not snowing at all. In a few weeks it might be. It doesn't snow very often in September," I told him.

"I'm deciding on what to wear, that's why I'm asking. Do you have a dresser stand?"

"Ansel—yes, I have that. Don't worry about anything until you get here."

"You don't sound anything like yourself. Have you changed that much without me?"

"You're going to meet a whole different person," I said, teasing him. "Finish packing your bags. I don't want you missing your bus."

"I'll get there an hour or so before."

"And I'll leave right now," I told him.

"And you'll leave right now," he said playfully. "See you after, Jack."

"I'll see you."

I put the phone away. I felt myself crying the way the standpipe at the Norman Bauer bridge does, moving down my face and meeting up at the corners of my mouth. From the nearest drawer, I found a drawing pencil and piece of paper—tearing it in two halves, I began writing out the phone call, making note of even the quiet rustling leaves outside. I couldn't remember a life apart from Maisie Kenton, and I certainly never wanted to forget one. I read it many times over, increasing the tightness in my jaw when I did, and then I deemed every line insignificant. I tore the whole thing into pieces that fell in a mess on the floor. When I was picking them up, I cut my finger on one of the paper's ends, and a tiny amount of blood surfaced. I wiped it against my sweater, reminding myself that if you never bleed at even the very smallest things, you must not bleed at all.

I got myself dressed. I wore my favorite blue long sleeve dress shirt, and my favorite grey jacket over it. I felt nervous knowing I was going to see Ansel again, and suddenly very concerned about how I looked from various angles. I stared at the bathroom mirror contemplating—would Ansel recognize me again? I cut my hair different, though I present myself all the very same. Was he going to walk right by me at the bus station, forgetfully clean of snow dancing and at times every so often, after dark especially, colorless swearing? I knew him every day for a long time, but I don't know that he ever paid very well attention.

I began pacing upstairs, harassing the floor boards apparently, until I got the idea that I should invite Marigold to the bus station along with me. I went downstairs and called her.

"But you haven't ever mentioned him before," Marigold said. We were at the bus station seeking distraction. Marigold had bought us coffees that we finished pretty quickly.

"I didn't know if he was dead or anything. I wasn't going to mention him in case he was," I said. "I couldn't find any good reason in doing that."

"You seem to admire him, though," she said.

"How's that?"

"You called him tough. I've never heard you use that word before." I laughed sort of.

"That's because he's very tough. He had frostbite in his pinky finger when he was a little kid and he can't bend it any way, but he never told me that until I asked. He never tells you anything if you don't ask. Actually— I don't even know what he was at Macauley for. He never mentioned why."

"What do you believe?" she asked. I couldn't answer right away. How, most of anything at all, did I not know why Ansel got sent to Macauley?

"Oh, I don't know, really," I said.

"Was he mad?"

"I don't think so. I wouldn't have ever asked him that anyway. It's impolite."

"Oh, I'm sorry. I didn't mean it badly or anything."

"I know you didn't."

There was a pause.

"Were him and Maisie in love?" Marigold asked.

"How would you define love?" I said. She grasped my hand.

"For myself—it's someone I wouldn't ever let go of."

"Oh, well, then yes, they were in love. At some point."

There was another pause. She was still holding my hand.

"Did you ever love Ben?" I asked.

"I could have loved him my whole life," she said. "I just won't get to."

"It doesn't matter if somebody's dead. You can still love them anyway," I said. "I know I won't ever stop loving my mom."

Suddenly, then, from across the station's platform, I saw red boat sails hanging free in the wind. I kept my eyes on them until they changed into a girl's regular hair.

Margot was there—and she was leaving. My feet were a part of the floor's material, it seemed, and Marigold hadn't yet let my hand go, so I couldn't do anything to stop her.

I watched her run along the station's platform until she passed from my sight forever.

And I gave Marigold's hand a little squeeze while I did.

My heart beat the previous ways.

"Could we be dreaming?" Marigold asked.

"Dreaming what?" I said.

"The entire past year. What if it was all a very terrible dream?" My lip quivered at the thought.

I bumped my leg against hers, and squeezed her hand another time.

I stared at my coffee cup, troubled by the remaining tea leaves and the very thought of everything. One day I'm going to stop thinking forever if I can.

"Did you ever love Ben?" Marigold said.

"I might have loved him a long time ago, but if you had asked me, I would have absolutely refused. I didn't know how to love anyone the correct ways."

"What's the right way?" she asked.

"Oh, I couldn't say. Have you any idea?"

"Not even a single one."

Eventually, Marigold let go of my hand, and she kissed my cheek after she did.

"Would you ever go away?" I asked her.

"Only if we were going together," she said. We both smiled.

Ansel's bus arrived at the station exactly on time. I saw him watching from the window. He waved at me, smiling in this very big way—reminding me about where I knew that expression from. I couldn't believe it. We were apart so long that I'd forgotten what his expressions looked like.

The bus doors opened. I hid my shaking hands in my pockets as they did.

A very small number of people came out before him. There was a man smoking a cigarette, holding this little girl's little hand, and a younger boy with pretty straight hair following closely behind them. A woman in a leather fur coat stepped out with a carry-on bag hanging down from her arm, followed by this older guy that had two suitcases.

After that came Ansel, and his eyes so notably green. He looked the very same. His hair was cut regularly short at length. Neatly combed over were his golden bangs in red, yellow coloring. I only noted one different thing about him, and that was a little scar below his left eye.

I felt myself getting emotional already, pulling him in.

"It's good to see you again," he said. "I love the same things I always did."

"Thanks for coming back," I told him.

"I was always going to," he said.

I pulled back to look at him.

"Where did you get that from?" I asked, feeling the scar just below his eye. It felt brand new.

He dismissed my inquiry.

"Are you Marigold?" he said, letting go from the hug. "I've heard everything about you."

"So have I," she said. Ansel looked at me, smiling.

"That's awfully encouraging," he said.

"Do you have a suitcase?" I asked him.

"Oh, yeah! I would've forgotten if you hadn't said anything!"

He ran back onto the bus very fast, almost falling over himself when he did. Marigold and I waited for him to get back.

"How do you feel?" she said.

"Fine, actually," I said. "He's just the same as he was."

"Can you forgive him?" she asked.

"Oh, well—yes, probably. I have nothing better to do."

I feel love is much easier anyway.

Ansel came running back down the bus steps, carrying a light brown leather suitcase in his right hand. Later, while helping him unpack in my bedroom, he mentioned that Maisie had bought it for him as a birthday gift.

"Was it your birthday?" I asked, realizing I didn't know his goddamn birthday. He made it even worse after.

"Today is, yes," he said.

"What do you mean, today's your birthday?" I paused. "How come I didn't know that?"

"I don't know if I ever said it before. It's nothing serious anyway."

I moved to sit closer to him.

"I'm sorry, I should have known that," I said.

"I won't hold it above your head or anything. Besides, I have everything I need already. I don't need anything more."

I leaned my forehead against his own.

"You're a gem," I said.

"I know that. You've told me that before."

"I just never want you to forget."

"I won't ever have the capability living with you. Are you positive your dad won't mind?"

"He won't at all," I told him, sitting back against my bed. "He's very easygoing. I love him that way."

Coming from inside Ansel's suitcase, I noticed a shiny glaring all of a sudden. "Ansel—what is that?"

I sat forward to look inside, finding a silver horseshoe when I did.

My mind went back, months ago, to the story Ansel told me about his little brother carrying a horseshoe around everywhere. Do you remember it?

"What's that from?" I asked him.

"Oh, I've always had that," he said, plainly. He kept putting his things away into my dresser's bottom drawer.

"Who gave you it?"

"My mother," he said. "She did horse riding."

"Is it like the one your brother had?"

He stared at me confused.

"I don't have a brother," he said.

"What do you mean?"

"I never had a brother."

"But that story you told me—you said your brother would carry a horseshoe around wherever he'd go. You said he broke a kid's nose using it."

"I don't know why I would've said that."

"So did you make that whole thing up?"

"Oh, well, not completely. I broke someone's nose with this horseshoe before. He goddamn deserved it, too."

His face showed not a small difference in expression having just revealed this. Meanwhile, I couldn't believe it. I traced my fingernail from being nervous.

From the very start, the boy in the horseshoe story was Ansel.

"We have to go in a moment," I said to him. My clock radio had given noisy warning. "Maisie's going to be here in a minute. Are you going to wear that?" He was wearing a red sleeved shirt and jeans.

"Would that be alright?" he said.

"On a regular day, yes, but not for a vigil. You'll have to change quickly."

In my closet, I found a very thin black sweater Ansel could wear. I gave it to him, and taking off his red shirt, he threw it onto my bedroom floor.

I noticed he must have gotten stronger in his time away.

Marigold parked a street over from Harwich Boulevard. We couldn't get any closer because there was already so much parking occupied. Westley Reid was popular, yes, goddamn, but it seemed that all of Cradock was there—and for what exactly? He killed his girlfriend in front of everybody. How do you admire someone who's inspired so much harm? You make the curtains dirty, put them on and wear them out.

We got out of the car and started walking to Harwich Boulevard.

"You look nice," Marigold said to me. "And so do you, Ansel. I like that sweater." She gave me a smile.

"I don't know how I feel doing this," I said. "Last time I was at Westley's house was the same night Ben died. My heart's beating so fast about it."

Marigold adjusted the strap of her dress.

"You were going to have to do it eventually," she said. "You can't avoid everything forever."

"I could if I wanted anyway," I said.

"I'd never speak to you again if you did that. Your heart's soft, Jack, not so much faint. Don't get that confused."

"When did you ever get so smart?" I asked.

"When you weren't paying attention," she said, taking my hand and pulling me aside from a car going across the street that I hadn't noticed coming.

"I didn't know you two were romantics," Ansel cut in. "You're practically dancing together."

We both laughed at him. At some point he was the funniest person in the room.

Westley's house was dressed in green and yellow ribbon. A woman was passing out bracelets of the same colors. I'd assume they were Westley and Casey's favorites if I had to.

Ansel's bracelet snapped immediately after him putting it on.

"Can I have another?" he asked the lady.

"You can just have mine," I said, offering him it, though mine broke at the very same rate.

"How cheaply were these made?" Ansel said.

"That's not important at all," Marigold interrupted. "We didn't come for the jewelry."

"I wouldn't call it that anyway," he said.

"Ansel, stop," I told him. He still hadn't learned any good manners.

Marigold's name came from a small company of girls by the front door. When I looked over at them, I saw it was the whole cheerleading team, dolled up in their face makeup and glittery outfits. Even if you explained it to me like I was dim-witted, I still would never understand how that wardrobe was necessary for this kind of thing.

Marigold went over to them.

"Who are they?" Ansel asked.

"That's the cheerleading girls," I said.

"Was Casey Morris a cheerleader?"

"Oh—she was the goddamn captain," I told him.

"Maisie said Casey told everybody she was a slut in the eighth grade."

"She kept that up well into high school, too. I don't know that she ever stopped anyway."

"Bitter ending—isn't that funny?" he said, hitting my shoulder.

"You've got to behave, Ansel."

"Relax, Jack. I'll be good." He put out his right pinky finger and promised.

When eventually Marigold came back over, I asked her if the cheerleading team was doing a special performance or anything.

She answered no.

The candle wax was running down through my hands, making the candle difficult to hold.

"Do these last forever?" Ansel asked.

"It won't be much longer," I said to him, though I didn't know really. Surprisingly enough, this was my very first vigil. Ben never got so lucky as to have one.

I felt hot in my face being there again at Westley's house, as the water level had gotten low enough for drowned ships to float again. Every memory was resurfacing in little amusing ways reminding me that tragedy exists in everything at all. You can't escape it anyhow. You can run until your legs are tired, and the bottoms of your feet bleed from all of the broken glass you're trying so hard to leave behind, but right there—

in the far back place of your mind—you're being followed closely still. You'll only notice this at some time, though, when you think you've gotten away, and by then it's much too late to do anything. Enjoy yourself even in the darkest.

I gave Ansel my candle to hold.

"I'll be right back in a minute," I said, leaving him and Marigold and the whole world in the front yard. In noisy whispering, Marigold was calling behind me as I walked into Westley Reid's house.

I felt the floorboards creak as they did before, only this time I could actually hear them in their activity. It was quiet as best I can figure death would be.

I found my way up the stairs. At the very top remained the photograph of Westley as a little boy, smoking a candy cigarette. I ran my finger over the frame, collecting dust on my fingertip when I did. Would they ever bother to clean it?

Remembering Westley's room was at the end of the hallway on the right, I found myself there in time. I opened the door and walked inside. I didn't remember it any differently.

I noticed first his bed left unmade, and then the multiple wastebaskets by his nightstand overfilled with lots of paper things. Some of the trash had fallen out onto the floor, and so I bent down and picked it up. After I did that, I made his bed. I expected no one was going to ever again anyway. I sat down on it once I finished.

Outside the window, I saw all the candle lights.

Inside my head is a perfect world. I close my eyes and Ben sits down on the bed beside me. He makes himself comfortable.

"Can you stay long?" I ask him.

"I'll have to get home soon," he says.

"Oh, that's alright," I tell him. "I still love you, though."

"Did you ever stop?"

"At one point, I did. I was a little angry. I just didn't expect you'd have to go."

"I know that. I'm sorry I did."

I look at him and he's a little kid again like how when I first met him, and he's crying like how little kids do. I hug him, though, and he grows up in my hands. He's taller than me now, and he's stronger than I'll ever be, and his heart beats with all the speed in the world. I never want to let him go, but my mom's voice is there all of a sudden, and she's telling me how when I was younger I'd never let the tree branch from the backyard go. Suddenly I don't feel his heart beating anymore, and I know what's necessary.

And I let him go.

The floor behind me creaks, wakening me. I opened my eyes.

"Just give me a minute, please," I said, without looking back to see who it was. I assumed it would be Marigold anyway. But the voice wasn't hers.

"It's a goddamn mess in here," Ansel said. "At least the bed's made."

"I did that," I told him. I was crying a little.

"Oh, well, of course you did," he said. He made his way over next to me. "Maisie told me about Ben and what happened. I'm sorry, Jack."

"You don't have to be. It's not your fault or anything."

"I'm still very sorry. It's a terrible thing. I wish you had told me yourself."

"Why, what would you have said?"

"Probably nothing at all. You and I work better when I'm just listening anyway."

I felt a tear go down my face. I wiped it away after noticing.

"Do you know you're a wonderful person?" Ansel said. "I've always enjoyed just sitting with you, listening. You have a very good decency."

"I don't know if I believe that very well," I told him.

"What, do you think you're a bad person?" he asked.

"I think I've done barely enough to be deemed good. I suppose I've told a few too many lies to believe that."

"And what lies have you told exactly?"

I looked at him and when I did, I thought about you, actually, and this very extensive lie I've kept up that you might not believe even if I admitted it. I don't know if you'd like me any after either.

"I killed Ben," I said. I started crying harder. "He was taking me home. Did Maisie mention that? And I never loved my mom enough to save her. And I loved Maisie Kenton too much. And for some reason I feel bad for Westley Reid even though he shot Casey. And I told Phoebe that I didn't remember anything when I do remember everything that's ever happened my whole life. I just wanted her to stop asking about anything at all. I just wanted the whole world to go quiet forever. I thought I could make that happen."

I had to stop talking because I was crying too much. At first, when I did, Ansel didn't say anything. Sometime after, though, he said, "We can make that happen."

My face must have shown I didn't understand.

"We can let the world go totally quiet," he said. "Just have it be you and me all the way down. We don't have to say anything to anyone ever again." Though I was crying still, I smiled halfway. Ansel could make you do that even at the most awful times.

He didn't say anything after that. As he'd suggested, he let the world go totally quiet. Falling slantwise, it stayed that way for a little while. I stared out the window at the plenty of lights and decided having Ansel at my side was going to make for a good life.

And I was going to allow that to happen.

Back outside, I held Marigold's hand. She rested her head on part of my shoulder—the part that could hold everything—and we listened as Westley Reid's parents thanked everybody for coming by. Casey's parents stayed away to the side and never said anything the whole night. From just a brief glance at them, I saw their sadness quite simple as they weren't hiding it very easy anyway. I felt very bad, awful—really, that Casey was dead. I knew they were feeling the same, and from my observation, wishing the same—that we could only feel so much at once, and forget past things effortlessly when desired. Memory's not so bad when it's good, but it seems rarely ever so good anymore. Would you consider it a gift—remembering? Or the most terrible thing we're capable of?

Eventually the candles burned out as all things do, and the magnificence of night against the streetlamps developed very good shadows of Marigold, Ansel and me. I watched them dance along the street as we made our way back to the car. Watching them, for some reason, I felt so young again. Could it be, I thought, that all this time I just needed my friends and their shadows dancing? Had I found a way to fix the suffering by dancing beside them? Could it ever be so easy?

I told myself yes.

At the end of Harwich Boulevard was the broken stop sign still. Marigold was the first to stop walking when we came upon it.

"Sometimes I hate him, you know," she said.

"Hate who?" I asked.

"Ben, sometimes, when I think about him."

"Why's that, though?"

"For trying to save the paper boy," she said. "If only he didn't save the paper boy." I looked away from the broken sign at her.

"He was dead already," I told her. "He couldn't have saved him even if he gave all his effort trying."

"Oh, Jack, don't say that, please. Just let me believe he could have."

"It's not anyone's job to save anybody," Ansel cut in. "I thought you both would know that already."

I waited for Marigold to respond to him, but she didn't, and I didn't either. Sadly, though, we both knew Ansel was right, and that the fantasy of saving everybody would forever be told just as it were—a fantasy. It's most important that you understand this now before you grow up and it's too late for understanding.

Marigold drove me and Ansel home. There were no songs that I recognized on the radio, but Ansel knew one of them apparently. I got to hear him sing a little. He said it was called "Touch of Grey." I liked it very much.

We said goodbye to Marigold. She told me she'd be back over some time in the morning to pick us up. In the morning we're going to the cemetery to put out flowers. It's going to be one year since my mom died tomorrow. I can't believe that.

I was looking in my pockets for my house key when my dad opened the front door.

"Hey, dad," I said. "Do you remember Ansel?" My dad looked at Ansel all over. Noticeably on his face, he was thinking where he knew him before. He'd only met him just one time, but I was hoping he remembered him anyway. My dad has a very good memory. Better than any novels I've ever read.

"Do you know him from school?" he asked.

"No, he was my roommate at Macauley," I told him. It didn't take him very long to remember after I said that. His face was bright.

"Ansel, yes! Those must be your bags upstairs. I was wondering whose they were."

"Were you in my bedroom?" I asked.

"Only putting your laundry away," he said regular as ever. From the way he said that, I wouldn't have thought anything more. Would you have? "Well, get in the house, before you let all the bugs in the neighborhood in."

I followed Ansel inside, and into the living room, where Phoebe was sitting on the couch for some reason.

"What's happening?" I said, looking at her and then back at my dad of course. I was awfully confused at the whole setting.

"You missed our session today," Phoebe said. "I wanted to see if you were alright." I had completely forgotten it was Monday!

"Oh, I'm sorry. I just had a lot going on," I told her. It wasn't necessarily dishonest or anything. I mean I did have the most going on today it seemed.

"It's frightening everything that happened with those two kids, Jack. Would you like to discuss it?"

I felt very uncomfortable all of a sudden, especially having Ansel there. I didn't want him seeing me in such a piteous way again. He may think I'm open to that one feeling only.

"What happened doesn't hardly involve me," I said. "I know it's awful what happened, yes, but it's not at all my concern or anything particular. Is this really why you've come the whole way to my house?"

I stared very angry at her. I could feel my hands just barely shaking.

"Jack, won't you sit down?" Phoebe said.

Shaking my head, I told her I'd prefer not to. I didn't feel at all tired enough for that anyway. Phoebe sighed at this.

"Can you be absolutely honest, Jack?" she asked all of a sudden, glaring at me, as though a table lamp in a holding room. "What do you remember from the past year?"

Sounding out that question by itself, I knew right away what had taken place while I was away at the vigil. While doing laundry, my dad must have found my journal in my room, and read the whole thing himself—had I left it on my desk? Halfway through, he must have realized Jack Boyd was a false name. If it was going to be anyone that made sense of anything it was going to be my dad. And I should've known that of course. He was always a very smart man.

I glanced at my dad, and oddly enough, I saw him as I always did. I thought how sad he looked, as though his eyes were overwhelmed by smoky flames spreading inside the house's empty air. Had the relationship of my hands set things carefully ablaze? For how long could I play this chess game without burning everything close to me? Moving the game piece was a lovely thought at first. Should I have kept it that way?

For a minute I stopped believing in anything.

And then I began crying.

I saw ahead of me every little thing covered in ash being cleaned, as though sugar on the countertop and not once luminous blazing things. I washed my fingernails dirty with the Earth under the sink after, and clipped them also. They were growing long.

Once I composed myself, I was able to admit everything. How we're goddamned from the very beginning with knowledge and the gift for remembering things. Wouldn't you agree so? We find tiny amusement in games at the arcade until the sound effects become too familiar, and you're realizing it's the same noise your mom's breathing device made. Your favorite movie has a car accident scene and you notice the broken glass is a little blinding. You recollect the pieces again, and during that, you find your hand never healed the first time.

Dying's a curiosity I have. Did I mention that already? When I got home the day my mom died, I sat by her empty bed for a while. And I thought about how she won't ever sleep in it again, yet there's an imprint from where she did before. On her nightstand were her things, and she was just using them the day before. I felt the creasing of the bed sheets from where she slept, and knew this wasn't going to be easy. I just couldn't have expected it to get even worse.

Ben died several days later. I've told you everything there is about that. I explained to Phoebe that I only lied so I could sort the whole thing out. I wanted you to understand he was a good person. The newspaper headings only said he killed the paperboy, but I was in the car beside him that night, and he didn't mean to anyway. If I only could let the whole world know that, I would. I'd get on every housetop and scream it at them below if I had to. But writing was the most accessible thing I could do. They don't let me go very high places anyway. From what happened, I understand.

I should let you know my name isn't Jack Boyd. Jack Boyd was the paperboy a year ago. I only knew his name from the posters they hung up in all places once he went missing. He wasn't ever found or anything still today. And they hired a new paperboy that ended up dying the same night my best friend did. Just don't ever become a paperboy. It's the worst thing you can ever do apparently.

My name is Norman Bauer instead. Days after my best friend died, I jumped from the town's bridge into the flowing river current below. The evening was drawing close when I did it, and the sun was settling blue upon the water—the very type that gets you so easily confused. I didn't set out for the bridge having plans to jump or anything. I believe that as I held onto the bridge's railing I realized the world no longer fit in my hands. It had grown far too heavy to hold myself, and there are limits to carrying things. I feel sorry if you understand exactly what I mean.

I used all my body's strength to lift myself onto the railing. A couple of people walked by, I remember, but nobody said anything. Nobody ever says anything until you jump, and so that's what I did—though I only heard one scream, and the voice belonged to me in my head. Beneath the water I felt whole again, as though I could avoid the suffering forever. Until my head began screaming outrageous things at me, and I found myself back in the garden with my mom. She was wearing a big white hat pulling tulips. Everything felt extraordinarily bright, yellow and green.

She showed me a very perfect looking tulip.

Admiring it, she said, "I can feel this one's still breathing."

"How do you know that?" I asked. She picked a petal off and gave me it. Right away, oddly enough, I could feel its heart beating.

She resumed pulling flowers, setting the prettiest ones aside to be sold later.

"Tulips can live a very long time," she said. "Even in the coldest point of winter. That's why they're my favorite. And they smell delightful also." She brought one up to her nose, breathing in the smell of all things soft honey and lovely.

I went to pull a flower of my own, but when I did, it wouldn't move from the dirt or anything. Was I not quite strong enough? My mom noticed my trying very hard.

"Oh, well, they're not for you, Norman," she said. She reached over and pulled the very same flower out from the ground as though it were cut already. She handed it to me after. Right when she did, the whole thing wilted in my hand, scattering dust everywhere.

"But it's unfair," I said. "I don't want to go back."

"I know that, Norman, but your dad would miss you far too much. He couldn't ever brave it all by himself," she said.

"But what if I can't either?" I said.

"Oh, yes, well, that's why you have each other."

Looking at me, my mom ran her fingers all through my hair, neatening it for my going back, and for the very last time ever, she smiled at me. I won't see her again for a very long time.

I don't remember anything more after that, except waking up in a hospital bed. I read in the newspaper my body surfaced on the river's side not very long after, and somebody did that whole breathing technique to save my life, but they never said who. I suppose it means nothing to be a hero.

I spent a week in the hospital before going to Macauley. My heart felt very small the whole time. I kept the window blinds shut, and didn't speak to anybody. Every night I cried as much as possible just so I could get sleep. I'd never felt so alone in my whole life yet, and then I arrived at Macauley, and met Ansel.

And he liked having the blinds open.

I finished talking, and as though a spectacular change occurred, nobody said anything more at all. The house grew absolutely quiet. Even the very thought of everything stopped making noise. I found the silence most pleasant. Ansel couldn't let that happen forever, though, of course.

"Apparently you've got some brilliant mind," was the only thing he said. I smiled at him, and breathed relief for the first time in the longest time ever. I didn't cry anyhow, instead I thought I could someday be happy again. I would just have to live in my skin for a little while first, and organize the piles of clothes in my room, too. Ansel said he could help me do that, though. I would just have to let him of course.

Phoebe and I agreed to start meeting twice a week. She also said I should continue writing anyway, and so I'm going to. I'll have to find something new to write about, though, or I'll get terribly bored of doing so. You must know that I get bored easy by now.

Ansel was in the bathroom earlier, cleaning his teeth, when my dad came into my room. He leaned against the doorframe.

"Maybe you and I can get the kitchen window fixed sometime. It's going to be a cold winter," he said. "And I could get your mom's bike down from the attic, so maybe you, Ansel and I could go biking."

"I don't know if Ansel knows how to ride a bike," I said.

"He'll get to know how—well, that's only if he's going to stay."

"He's going to stay," I said, smiling at him. He smiled back. And when he said I love you, I told him the very same.

When I first started writing you, my whole bedroom desk arrangement, I worried, was too ordinary a place to put my life's work out. But I'm sitting here now, and my best friend is asleep in my bed, and the whole city's asleep in their beds, and the world seems just quiet enough to handle again. From the bathroom, I can hear the faucet dripping a little at a time, and from outside I can hear the leaves whistling.

I require nothing more.

<u>Chapter 11</u>:

From the Window Glared the Sunrise Over the Great Black Sky

Early this morning before the sun got up, I found my dad in the kitchen fixing the window above the sink. Every overhead light was on accompanying him in this activity.

"What are you doing awake?" I asked him.

"Fixing the window," he said. "We shouldn't have left it broken for so long."

I corrected him. "It wasn't very long. Just over a year."

"Even so," he said. "Did you sleep well?"

"Did you sleep at all?" I asked him. He wasn't looking at me. He was very focused on the window apparently.

"For an hour or so I did."

I found a tall water glass in the cabinet and used the faucet to fill it all the way. I had come downstairs for water to begin anyway. Finding my dad was just another thing that happened. I sat down at the table after.

"It's one year already," I said, taking a big sip from my glass.

"I know," he said, fascinated by the very same part of the broken window still. He wasn't getting anywhere, I mean. His defeat was obvious in his shaking hands.

"Maybe you should stop that. Do you know what you're doing anyway?" I said.

He inhaled sharply and began putting his things away into his tool bag. He seemed in a hurry, doing that, and so I knew exactly what was going on.

"Could you sit down?" I asked him. "I'll get you water."

Once he sat down, and I got him water, he exhaled. On top of the table's surface, I held his hand as he cried a little while. We stayed that way for a little while, too, when eventually, from the window glared the sunrise over the great black sky. And I knew we'd be alright. We just had to get to the warmer seasons again.

Ansel woke up sometime after, and he came downstairs and made everyone coffees. For some reason, it was the best pot of coffee I've ever had in my whole life. I don't know what Ansel did to accomplish that, but one day I'll figure it out if I can, and I'll let you know of course.

We got dressed after. I let Ansel wear one of my nicest vests. It's green and white. Marigold came by at around ten o'clock to pick us up. I opened the passenger side door, and when I did, taking place in my seat was a bouquet of flowers. They were white tulips.

"Where did you get them?" I asked.

"I found them out in the field by the park," she said. "I spent a while looking."

I smiled at her, and placed the bouquet in my lap for safekeeping. It wasn't a very long ride to the cemetery of course, but I didn't want them falling anywhere. When we got there, I breathed in heavily. I whispered to myself nothing and stared out the window at the trees moving in the most exciting ways. If you don't ever know the time of year, the trees will give it away if nothing else does first.

Marigold showed me Ben's gravestone, and seeing it, oddly enough, felt very nice. Knowing Ben was plenty safe covered by the dirt was comforting in some way. Flowers grow at any rate, from dirt all the same.

Marigold put one very pretty, bright red rose on his grave, and then we made it over to my mom's grave. I started crying instantly. Nobody said anything the whole time. I just thought I'm going to miss them both my whole life, for however long I'm capable of missing somebody.

I bent down and set the bouquet of flowers neatly on the ground. When I got back up, Ansel put his arm around my shoulder, and Marigold held my hand. I told you once that I was at the worst goddamn advantage of anybody alive, but I am so lucky to have my best friends.

I can hear the songbirds, mom.

And they are so beautiful.